Robin Hood: His Book

The Red has it, the Red, the Red! so the crowd shouted

Robin Hood his book

by Eva March Tappan
Author of 'In the Days of Alfred the Great' etc.

illustrated by Charlotte Harding

Biography of Eva March Tappan

Eva March Tappan was born on 26th December 1854 in Blackstone, Massachusetts, America. She is well known as a factual as well as fictional writer, but spent her early career as a teacher. Tappan was the only child of Reverend Edmund March Tappan and Lucretia Logée, and received her education at the esteemed Vassar College. This was a private coeducational liberal arts college, in the town of Poughkeepsie, New York, from which she graduated in 1875. Here, Tappan was a member of Phi Beta Kappa, the oldest honour society for the liberal arts and sciences, widely considered as the nations most prestigious society. She also edited the *Vassar Miscellany,* a college publication.

After leaving her early education, Tappan began teaching at Wheaton College, one of the oldest institutions of higher education for women in the United States, founded in 1834 and based in Norton, Massachusetts. She taught Latin and German here, from 1875 until 1880, before moving on to the Raymond Academy in Camden, New Jersey where she was associate Principal until 1894. Tappan also received a graduate degree in English Literature from the University of Pennsylvania. This allowed her to pursue her first love, that of reading and writing, and she taught as head of the English department at the English High School at Worcester, Massachusetts.

It was only after this date that Tappan began her literary career, writing about famous characters in history, often aimed at educating children in important historical themes and epochs. Some of her better known works include, *In the Days of William the Conqueror* (1901) and *In the Days of Queen Elizabeth* (1902), *The Out-of-Door Book* (1907), *When Knights Were Bold* (1911) and *The Little Book of the Flag* (1917). Tappan never married, being a happy singleton, and died on 29th January 1930, aged seventy-five.

PREFACE

IN all English history, be it true or be it legendary, no hero stands out in bolder, clearer relief than the outlaw Robin Hood. Was he a real Englishman the tales of whose achievements are based upon real deeds? Is the name but a chance selection around which clusters the English portion of those legends of strength and valor that have come down to us from the earlier days? Is Robin but a personified reminiscence of the Maytime games and the restless joy that is felt at the coming of springtime? What does it matter? Why should one care in which of three kingly reigns a veritable " Robert Hood " may perchance have lived? Far more worthy of regard is it that just as the stories of Cœur de Leon embody the early English idea of the perfect knight, the hero of the nobles, so do the ballads of Robin picture the free and sturdy yeoman, the hero of the people.

Robin is a ranger of the forest, an outlaw, not for crime as we count crime, but for shooting the

Preface

king's deer, a " naughtiness " for which there was
no atonement save that of the gallows tree.   He
is no rebel, he loves his king, and he is a devout
attendant at church whenever the absence of the
proud sheriff will permit. Of gentle birth is
Robin, but far more admirable than the servility
that "dearly loves a lord" is the submission of
his good bowmen, not to their master's noble de-
scent nor even to his physical strength, for in a
fair contest many a one among them is more than
his match, but to some intellectual quality which
makes him superior to themselves, and calls forth
their unquestioning obedience.

Robin is not the embodiment of the determined
resistance to injustice that brought about Magna
Charta; still less is the stout-hearted ranger an
exponent of that aimless feeling that "the time is
out of joint" which came to the surface in the
Peasants' Revolt; and yet he stands for a crude
lurch of thought toward reform in his scorn of
the luxurious nobles and mercenary bishops, and
his honest friendliness for the simple parish priests
who represented to many a one among the com-
mon folk all that he knew of the goodness and
charity of the church.   Robin is more just, even

Preface

in his hatred, than many a modern agitator, for, though he abhors the nobles as a class, he is ready to give most generously to aid the knight who in sorest distress chances to fall into the hands of the dreaded outlaw. He robs with complacence the greedy sheriff who hangs men "but to get their gold and gear," but he delights in tossing a silver shilling over the shoulder of the hard-working husbandman at the plough.

His influence upon the English nation can hardly be estimated. Bishop Latimer was, indeed, wrathfully indignant that some villagers had locked the church door and gone to the greenwood to celebrate Robin's day instead of assembling to listen to the pastoral admonitions; but for all the good bishop's displeasure, Robin's influence was a sound one. Faithfulness to the king, devotion to the church, love of the out-of-doors, willingness to aid whoever is in need, bravery in redressing the wrongs of the helpless — these are not qualities of the hero of romance whose example will lead the people very far astray. The king has become less arbitrary, the church has waxed more thoughtful of her humbler children, hours of labor have been shortened that the toilers may have more of leisure

Preface

for the joys of meadow and forest and stream, the moneybags of the rich have opened to aid the poor, even without the compulsory appeal of the highway robber, and the wrongs of the helpless have been more surely redressed by other means than the sword; but the spirit that reveals itself in this growing thoughtfulness of one for another is the same spirit whose crude manifestation centuries ago inspired the ballads of Robin and his followers, and their merry life in the good greenwood.

In the olden times there were heroes indeed. One generation vanished, another and another, but the hero endured. Every year his glory increased. Every deed of bravery was magnified, every act of kindness shone the brighter as the days went by. Happy was the man who found a singer of ballads as the herald of his greatness. To a people simple, untravelled, unlearned, the ballad-maker was at once poet, musician, and man of the world. To him, wonted as he was to read the feelings of men from their faces, the thoughts of his hearers were as open as those of children. Straight into their eyes he looked as he touched his harp. He sang to one group and then to

Preface

another.   The frankness of their criticism, their eager applause, and their breathless interest were his inspiration.   Well might he sing song after song, coming nearer every time to the hearts of his eager listeners, every time unconsciously moulding his ballad as they themselves would have it to be. Was it his or was it theirs? It was the heart of the people set to the music of the poet.

As in the "Old Ballads in Prose," so in this rendering of some of the Robin Hood legends I have not scrupled to wander away from the exact incident and to add that story between the lines which the simple words of the ballad have brought to me without effort or searching of my own.

EVA MARCH TAPPAN.

Worcester, Mass.

CONTENTS

LIST OF ILLUSTRATIONS

List of Illustrations

ROBIN HOOD

HIS BOOK

I

ROBIN AND THE MERRY LITTLE OLD WOMAN

"Monday I wash and Tuesday I iron,
Wednesday I cook and I mend;
Thursday I brew and Friday I sweep,
And baking day brings the end."

SO sang the merry little old woman as she sat at her wheel and spun; but when she came to the last line she really could not help pushing back the flax-wheel and springing to her feet. Then she held out her skirt and danced a gay little jig as she sang, —

"Hey down, down, an a down!"

She curtseyed to one side of the room and then to another, and before she knew it she was curtseying to a man who stood in the open door.

"Oh, oh, oh!" cried the merry little old woman. "Whatever shall I do? An old woman ought to sit and spin and not be dancing like a young girl. Oh, but it 's Master Robin! Glad am I to set eyes on you, Master Robin. Come in, and I 'll throw my best cloak over the little stool for a cushion. Don't be long standing on the threshold, Master Robin."

"It 'll mayhap come to pass that I 'll wish I had something to stand on," said Robin, grimly, " for the proud bishop is in the forest, and he 's after me with all his men. It 's night and day that he 's been following me, and now he 's caught me surely. You 've no meal chest, have you, and you 've no press, and you 've no feather-bed, that 'll hide me? There 's but the one wee bit room, and there 's not even a mousehole."

The little woman's heart beat fast. What could she do?

" I mind me well of a Saturday night," said she, "when I 'd but little firewood and it was bitter cold, that you and your good men brought me such fine logs as the great folk at the hall don't have; and then you came in yourself and gave me a pair of shoon and some brand-new hosen, all soft and fine and woolly — I don't believe the king himself has such a pair — oh,

Master Robin, I've thought of something. Give me your mantle of green and your fine gray tunic, and do you put on my kirtle and jacket

and gown and tie my red and blue kerchief over your head — you gave it to me yourself, you did, it was one Easter Day in the morning — and do you sit down at the wheel and spin. See, you put your foot on the treadle *so*, to turn the wheel, and you twist the flax with your fingers *so*. Don't you get up, but just turn the wheel and grumble and mumble to yourself."

It was not long before the bishop and all his men came riding up to the little old woman's house. The bishop thrust open the door and called: —

" Old woman, what have you done with Robin Hood ? " but Robin sat grumbling and mumbling at the wheel and answered never a word to the proud bishop.

" She 's mayhap daft," said one of the bishop's men. " We 'll soon find him ; " and in a minute he had looked up the chimney and behind the dresser and under the wooden bedstead.   Then he turned to the corner cupboard.

" You 're daft yourself," said the bishop, " to look in that little place for a strong man like Robin." And all the time the spinner at the wheel sat grumbling and mumbling.   It was a queer thread that was wound on the spool, but no one thought of that.   It was Robin that they wanted, and they cared little what kind of thread an old woman in a cottage was a-spinning.

" He 's here, your Reverence," called the man who had opened the lower door of the corner cupboard.

[·4]

Robin Hood: His Book

"Bring him out and set him on the horse," ordered the bishop, "and see to it that you treat him like a wax candle in the church. The king's bidden that the thief and outlaw be brought to him, and I well know he'll hang the rogue on a gallows so high that it will show over the whole kingdom; but he has given orders that no one shall have the reward if the rascal has but a bruise on his finger, save that it came in a fair fight."

So the merry little old woman in Robin's tunic and Robin's green cloak was set gently on a milk-white steed. The bishop himself mounted a dapple-gray, and down the road they went.

It was the cheeriest party that one can imagine. The bishop went laughing all the way for pure delight that he had caught Robin Hood. He told more stories than one could make up in an age of leap-years, and they were all about where he went and what he did in the days before he became a bishop. The men were so happy at the thought of having the great reward the king had offered that they laughed at the bishop's stories louder than any one had ever laughed at them before. And as for the merry little old woman, she had the gayest time of all, though she had to keep her face muffled in her hood, and could n't laugh aloud the least bit, and could n't jump down from the great white horse and dance the gay little jig that her feet were fairly aching to try.

While the merry little old woman was riding off with the bishop and his men, Robin sat at the flax-wheel and spun and spun till he could no longer hear the beat of the horses' hoofs on the hard ground. No time had he to take off the kirtle and the jacket and the kerchief of red and blue, for no one knew when the proud bishop might find out that he had the wrong prisoner, and would come galloping back to the cottage on the border of the forest.

" If I can only get to my good men and true! " thought Robin; and he sprang up from the little flax-wheel with the distaff in his hand, and ran out of the open door.

All the long day had Robin been away from his bowmen, and as the twilight time drew near. they were more and more fearful of what might have befallen him. They went to the edge of the forest, and there they sat with troubled faces.

“I 've heard that the sheriff was seen but two days ago on the eastern side of the wood,” said Much the miller's son.

“And the proud bishop's not in his palace,” muttered William Scarlet. “Where he 's gone I know not, but may the saints keep Master Robin from meeting him. He hates us men of the greenwood worse than the sheriff does, and he 'd hang any one of us to the nearest oak.”

“He 'd not hang Master Robin,” declared Much the miller's son, “for the bishop likes good red gold, and the king 's offered a great reward for him alive and unhurt.” The others laughed, but in a moment they were grave again, and peered anxiously through the trees in one way and then in another, while nearer came the twilight.

“There are folk who say the forest is haunted,” said Little John. “I never saw anything, but one night when I was close to the little black pond that lies to the westward, I heard a cry that was n't from bird or beast, I know that.”

“And you did n't see anything ? ” asked Much the miller's son.

“No,” answered Little John, “but where there 's

a cry, there 's somewhat to make the cry, and it was n't bird or beast; I 'm as sure of that as I am that my name 's Little John."

" But it is n't," declared Friar Tuck. " You were christened John Little." No one smiled, for they were too much troubled about Robin.

" When I was a youngster," said William Scarlet, " I had an old nurse, and she told me that a first cousin of hers knew a woman whose husband was going through the forest by night, and he saw a witch carrying a round bundle under her arm. It was wrapped up in a brown kerchief; and while he looked, the wind blew the kerchief away, and he saw that the round bundle was a man's head. The mouth of it opened and called, ' Help! help! ' He shot an arrow through the old witch, and then he said to the head, ' Where do you want to go? Whose head are you ? ' The head answered, ' I 'm your head, and I want to go on your shoulders.' Then he put up his hand, and, sure enough, his own head was gone, and there it lay on the ground beside the dead witch with the arrow sticking through her. He took up the head and set it on his shoulders. This was the story that he told when he came back in the morning, but no one knew whether really to believe it all or not. After that night he always carried his head a bit to one side, and some said it was because he had n't set it back quite straight; but there are some folk that won't believe anything unless they see it themselves, and they said he had had a drink or two more than he should and that he took cold in his neck from sleeping with his head on the wet moss."

"Everybody knows there are witches," said William Scarlet, "and folks say that wherever they may be through the day, they run to the forest when the sun begins to sink, and while they're running they can't say any magic words to hurt a man if he shoots them."

"What's that?" whispered Much the miller's son softly, and he fitted an arrow to the string.

"Wait, make a cross on it first," said Little John.

Something was flitting over the little moor. The soft gray mist hid the lower part of it, but the men could see what looked like the upper part of a woman's body, scurrying along through the fog in some mysterious fashion. Its arms were tossing wildly about, and it seemed to be beckoning. The head was covered with what might have been a kerchief, but it was too dusky to see clearly.

"Don't shoot till it's nearer," whispered William Scarlet. "They say if you hurt a witch and don't kill her outright, you'll go mad forever after."

Nearer came the witch, but still Much the miller's son waited with his bow bent and the arrow aimed. The witch ran under the low bough of a tree, the kerchief was caught on a broken limb, and —

"Why, it's Master Robin!" shouted Much the miller's son. "It's Master Robin himself;" and so it was. No time had he taken to throw off the gray kirtle and the black jacket and the blue and red kerchief about his head; for as soon as ever he could no longer hear the tramp of the horses' hoofs, he had run with the distaff still in his hand to the shelter of the good greenwood and the help of his own faithful men and true.

Meanwhile the bishop was still telling stories of what he did before he was a bishop, and the men were laughing at them, and the merry little old woman was having the gayest time of all, even though she dared not laugh out loud.

Now that the bishop had caught Robin Hood he had no fear of the greenwood rangers; and as the forest road was much nearer than the high-way, down the forest road the happy company went. The merry little old woman had some-times sat on a pillion and ridden a farm beast from the plough; but to be on a great horse like this, one that held his head so high and stepped so carefully where it was rough, and galloped so lightly and easily where it was smooth — why, she had never even dreamed of such a magnificent ride. Not a word did she speak, not even when the bishop began to tell her that no gallows would be high enough to hang such a wicked outlaw. "You 've stolen gold from the knights," said he, "you 've stolen from the sheriff of Nottingham, and you 've even stolen from me. Glad am I to see Robin Hood — but what 's that?" the bishop cried. "Who are those men, and who is their leader? And who are you?" he demanded of the merry little old woman.

Now the little woman had been taught to order herself lowly and reverently to all her betters, so before she answered the bishop she slipped down from the tall white horse and made a deep curtsey to the great man.

"If you please, sir," said she, "I think it's Robin Hood and his men."

"And who are you?" he demanded again.

"Oh, I'm nobody but a little old woman that lives in a cottage alone and spins," and then she sang in a lightsome little chirrup of a voice:—

> "Monday I wash and Tuesday I iron,
> Wednesday I cook and I mend;
> Thursday I brew and Friday I sweep,
> And baking day brings the end."

I fear that the bishop did not hear the little song, for the arrows were flying thick and fast. The little old woman slipped behind a big tree, and there she danced her

> "Hey down, down, an a down!"

to her heart's content, while the fighting went on.

It was not long before the great bishop was Robin's prisoner, and ere he could go free, he had to open his strong leather wallet and count out more gold than the moon had shone on in the forest for many and many a night. He laid down the goldpieces one by one, and at every piece he gave a groan that seemed to come from the very bottom of his boots.

"That's for all the world like the cry I heard from the little black pond to the westward," said Little John. "It was n't like bird and it was n't like beast, and now I know what it was; it was the soul of a stingy man, and he had to count over and over the money that he ought to have given away when he was alive."

As for the merry little old woman, she was a prisoner too, and such a time as she had! First there was a bigger feast than she had ever dreamed of before, and every man of Robin's followers was bound that she should eat the bit that he thought was nicest. They made her a little throne of soft green moss, and on it they laid their hunting cloaks. They built a shelter of fresh boughs over her head, and then they sang songs to her. They set up great torches all round about the glade. They wrestled and they vaulted and they climbed. They played every game that could be played by torchlight, and it was all to please the kind little woman who had saved the life of their master.

Robin Hood: His Book

The merry little woman sat and clapped her hands at all their feats, and she laughed until she cried. Then she wiped her eyes and sang them her one little song.

The men shouted and cheered, and cheered and shouted, and the woods echoed so long and so loud that one would have thought they, too, were trying to shout.

By and by the company all set out together to carry the little old woman to her cottage. She was put upon their very best and safest horse, and Robin Hood would have none lead it but himself. After the horse came a long line of good bowmen and true. One carried a new cloak of the finest wool. Another bore a whole armful of silken kerchiefs to make up for the one that Robin had worn away. There were " shoon and hosen," and there was cloth of scarlet and of blue, and there were soft, warm blankets for her bed. There were so many things that when they were all piled up in the little cottage, there was no chance for one tenth of the men to get into the room. Those that were outside pushed up to the window and stretched their heads in at the door; and they tried their best to pile up the great heap of things

so she could have room to go to bed that night
and to cook her breakfast in the morning.

"And to-morrow's sweeping day," cried Robin.
"'Thursday I brew and Friday I sweep,' and
how'll she sweep if she has no floor?"

"We'll have to make her a floor," declared
Friar Tuck.

"So we will," said Robin. "There's a good man
not far away who can work in wood, and he shall
come in the morning and build her another room."

"Oh, oh!" cried the merry little old woman
with delight, "I never thought I should have
a house with two rooms; but I'll always care for
this room the most, for there's just where Master
Robin stood when he came in at the door, and
there's where he sat when he was spinning the
flax. But, Master Robin, Master Robin, did any
one ever see such a thread as you've left on
the spool!"

It was so funny that the merry little old woman
really could n't help jumping up and dancing

"Hey down, down, an a down!"

And then the brave men and true all said good-
night and went back to the forest.

II

ROBIN GOES A-FISHING

NE day when Robin was a young, young man, he said to his merrymen all : —

" I 've heard that a new air is good for a man, and I 'll to the sea for a while, to be a fisher."

" You 'll not be long away, will you, Master Robin ? " asked Little John.

" I 'll be back to chase the king's deer with you before the leaves are brown," answered Robin merrily.

" But, Master Robin, can you catch a fish ? " asked Friar Tuck.

" No man knows where his arrow may go," Robin answered wisely, " but he who can shoot a deer and save his neck from the sheriff ought to be able to catch a fish, for a fish-line makes no halters."

[16]

Robin Hood: His Book

So Robin set out for the seashore to become a fisher. When he came to Scarborough town, he said to himself: —

"Before you eat a fish, you must catch it, and before you catch it, it is well to have a place wherein to eat it. I 'll even find me an inn."

He wandered up and down the streets and looked at the inns. At last he lifted the big brass knocker at the door of a great house on the hill.

"Are you a captain?" demanded the serving-man. "We take no one but captains."

"No, I 'm not sure that I 'm a captain," replied Robin; and now he tried a tiny bit of a house at the foot of the hill.

"I don't really believe I could get myself into it," he thought, but he lifted the stone that hung by a cord and served as a knocker. A tiny maid-servant opened the door.

"Are you a cabin-boy?" asked the wee bit maid-servant. "We take no one but cabin-boys."

"No, I 'm not sure that I 'm a cabin-boy," answered Robin; and he went in search of some other house, where they took sailors that were neither captains nor cabin-boys.

Robin Hood: His Book

At last he came to one of gray stone. It was not so very large, and it was not so very small, so Robin knocked at the door.

"Is this an inn for fishermen?" he asked of the serving-girl.

"It's a house," said she, "and I'll ask the dame if it's an inn. She wants things the way she wants them, the dame does, and it's an inn if she says it is;" so off she ran to find her mistress.

Soon the dame herself came to the door.

"Who are you?" she asked Robin.

"I'm but a fisher lad," said he, "and I'm looking for an inn."

"What's your name?"

"Simon is a good name for a fisherman, and no one that I know is using it, so I'll just be Simon of the Sea."

"That's the strangest name that I ever heard. 'Of the sea' I know nothing about, but I'll call you Simon. I suppose you've come to get a place to work at an inn. What can you do, Simon?"

Now this Simon of the Sea was not really sure that he knew how to do anything but shoot deer, so he thought it was best to look as wise as possible and say, " I will do whatever you tell me to."

" Can you keep a basket full ? " queried the dame.

" Of venison ? " asked Robin cheerfully.

" The man's daft," said the dame, and she added, " No, stupid, of firewood."

" I think mayhap I could," said Robin meekly, for he began to feel as if there was no bed and no board for the man who was neither a captain nor a cabin-boy.

" I 'll take you," said the dame promptly. " I 'll pay you five shillings a month and your keep. You can go right to the shed and cut some wood for the basket."

So it was that Robin became a serving-man when he was only looking for an inn that was too small for captains and too large for cabin-boys. He stayed in the gray stone house a month and a day, then the good dame said to him : —

" Simon, it 's summer now, and the basket needs no wood.   What shall you do this summer ? "

" I 'd fain be a sailor," answered Robin, " but I 'm neither a captain nor a cabin-boy."

" There are men at sea that know less than the

cabin-boy and more than the captain," declared the dame. "What do you know?"

Robin was about to say, "I know how to shoot deer," but he remembered in time and said: —

"I know how to keep the basket full."

"So you do," declared the good dame heartily, "and a man who can keep the basket full can do anything. There's a vessel out here in the harbor and she's all my own. The planks are firm, the anchors are solid, and the ropes are good, and you shall go on her as a fisherman if you will."

The captain of the vessel was sent for, and he came down from the great house on the hill that took no one but captains.

"This man's to be a sailor on my ship," said the dame.

"What can he do?" asked the captain, scowling at the young man.

"He can fill a basket better than any other man that I ever saw," answered the dame. She smiled at Robin, but the captain scowled all the more and queried: —

"Young man, can you catch fish?"

"Of course he can," declared the dame promptly.

" If a man can fill a basket, can't he catch fish ? Every penny that he makes is going to be his own. Mind that, or you 'll sail no more of my ships."

" He 's welcome to it," growled the captain. " Get on board with you," he called to Simon ; but under his breath he muttered, " I 'll never sail another ship that a woman owns."

So it was that Robin became a fisherman. The next morning the captain pulled up his anchor and sailed out into the ocean.

" Furl the topsail," he ordered Robin ; but the new fisherman only stared at the captain.

" Climb up that pole, roll the white cloth into a bundle, and tie those strings together," roared the captain. " Can you understand that ? "

Robin furled the sail, but never before was a sail furled in such fashion. It was no wonder that all the sailors stood at the foot of the mast and grinned and chuckled and held their sides.

Soon Robin began to feel as if the top of his head was swinging off.

" I 'm very ill," he groaned. " Make me a bed that I may lie down in peace and die." The sailors laughed louder than ever, and even the captain stopped frowning and looked at him with a grim smile.

"You 'll get well," said he. "We can't stop to dig a grave just now. Get over there and haul the bowline taut."

Robin held fast to the side of the vessel and made his way to the nearest rope and hauled. It was the wrong rope, of course, and all sorts of things happened that ought not to have happened.

"Of all the stupid landlubbers!" cried the captain. "Get a fish-line and cast out, and see if you can fill a basket as well as the dame said you could."

Robin picked up a line and cast out just as he had seen the others do. The fish were plenty, and the man on his right and the man on his left brought them in by the score, but never a one did Robin catch. Hour after hour they sat there, pulling in the fish, and at last the man on his right asked, "Have you a hook on your line?" and the man on his left asked, "Have you a bait on your hook?"

"Indeed, I do not know," answered Robin; for the top of his head still felt as if it were swinging off.

Robin Hood: His Book

"Pull in your line," said the man on the right with a very wide grin. Robin pulled in his line. There was no bait on the hook and no hook on the line.

"Of all the stupid landlubbers!" cried the captain again. "You 'll have no part or lot in our catch, I tell you that. The dame said you could fill a basket equal to any man. What did you fill it with, I 'd like to know?"

"With wood," said Robin meekly.

"You 're naught but a woodenhead yourself," shouted the captain. "You can't haul a rope, you can't furl a sail, you can't catch a fish, and you can't even walk on the deck without falling down. You 're the most worthless fellow that ever held a fish-line."

"I wish I was in my own greenwood," thought Robin, "with my good merrymen around me, where there 's never a fishing-line, and where the ground lies still and does not pitch and toss and throw simple bowmen off their feet. Truly, the captain is right, and I 'm fit for naught."

Day after day Robin sat in the bow of the boat, for there was nothing that he could do, and the captain told him to keep out of the way.

Robin Hood: His Book

He gazed forlornly out over the sea; but at last his eyes brightened, and with all good cheer he called:—

"Captain, Captain, there's some kind of a boat out there, and there's a man on her with a bow."

"Some kind of a boat!" thundered the captain. "You don't know a man-of-war from a row-boat. That's a French man-of-war, and she'll take our fish and our vessel, and carry us all to France and throw us into prison. Woe is me, and woe is the day I was born."

"Don't be afraid, Captain," said Robin. "In my chest is my own good long-bow, and I'll shoot every Frenchman that comes near."

"Hold your peace," cried the captain in a rage. "We've enough to do without hearing your crack. You're naught but brag and boast, and 't would be best for us all to throw you overboard and lighten the vessel."

Nearer came the ship. The deck was black with Frenchmen. Their knives were in their hands, and they were ready to kill every Englishman on the fishing boat as soon as they could board it.

"I'll have one good shot before the captain throws me overboard," said Robin to himself, and he went down below to open his chest and take out his good yew-tree bow. The wind blew, and the deck pitched and tossed so beneath his feet that he could not well make his way to the bow of the ship.

"Captain, Captain," he cried, "I can't stand up, and I can't aim. Won't you tie me to the

mast, so I can shoot and I'll kill every Frenchman on board?"

"Yes, I'll tie you," said the captain, "and I'll
tie you well, so you'll be ready bound for them
when they come to take us to the French prisons;"
and he tied Robin fast and firm.

Then Robin shot, and the man at the bow of
the French man-of-war tumbled overboard with
an arrow through his heart. Robin shot again,
and the next man fell; so he shot, and he shot,
and never an arrow left his bow that did not kill
a Frenchman.

The captain and all his men stood around
Robin. Their eyes were open, and their mouths
were open, for never had they seen any shooting
like that.

"He fished without a hook."

"And he could n't furl a sail."

"And he could n't walk on the deck."

"And he did n't know the anchor from the
masthead."

So said the captain and his men, and all the
time Robin was firing as fast as he could fire, and
at every shot a Frenchman fell dead on the deck.
By and by he had but one arrow left.

"Captain," he asked, " is there another Frenchman?"

" Not another one," said the captain, "and
now we 'll go aboard."

The captain would let no one but himself
untie Robin from the mast.

"Simon," said he, "now come with me. Step
you warily, for the deck tilts and pitches, and I
would have naught befall you of harm or mis-
chance. You 'd best take my arm, and you 'll
walk the more safely."

They went aboard, and on the French man-of-
war they found twelve new barrels all standing in
a row, chained fast and firm to the deck.

"We 'll soon see what 's in them," said the
captain, and the ship's carpenter knocked off
the heads of the barrels. The men's eyes fairly
ached with the glitter, for every barrel was full to
the head with broad goldpieces, fresh and shining, just as they had come from the hand of the
coiner.

Now the captain was an honest man, and he
said, taking off his hat, " Master Simon, all this
is yours, for you won it with your own good
bow."

Robin Hood : His Book

" Nay, Captain," replied Robin. " Three barrels shall go to the kind dame; three barrels are for you and my good messmates on the vessel; three shall be for the poor folk of Scarborough town; and the other three I'll bear away with me to friends fast and true that live many leagues from Scarborough."

" We'll do no more fishing," declared the captain, "and we'll go back to the town, if so be, Master Simon, that it's your will."

" There's naught in all the world that I'd rather have than a bit of green turf beneath my feet," said Robin.

Then spoke the captain :—

" Sir Simon, the sailor's gear's not the thing for a rich man like you. Would you deign to wear my Sunday suit till you can send to London for what's better fitting so great a man ? "

Robin wore the captain's Sunday suit and had the captain's cabin all for his own. The cabin-boy served him on bended knee, and the captain came and offered his arm whenever they went to the table. " For," said he, " we must see that no touch of harm comes to a man like you."

Robin Hood: His Book

When they landed in Scarborough town, Robin gave three barrels of gold to the captain and the sailors, and three barrels to the parish priest for the poor folk of the town. He gave three barrels to the kind dame, and with the other three barrels he set out for the good greenwood.

Just as soon as he was well out of the town he put on his sailor gear, and when he came to the woods he walked down the forest road wheeling the gold and calling out : —

" Fish to sell, fine fish to sell ! "

His good men saw him coming, and they all ran out to meet him.

" The forest is but a lonely place without you, Master Robin," said Little John.

" The luck went with you," said William Scarlet, " for we 've had neither bishop nor sheriff for a dinner guest since you left us."

Then the three barrels of gold were opened, and there was a great rejoicing.

" But, Master Robin," asked Friar Tuck slyly, " did you catch any fish ? "

All this time the captain and the dame were talking together in the gray stone house in Scarborough town.

Robin Hood: His Book

"A woman always knows how to choose a man," declared the dame.

"Yes," said the captain; but he looked puzzled, and he went to the great house on the hill to think the matter over.

III

ROBIN HOOD AND LITTLE JOHN

"MASTER," said William Scarlet, "here 's a rare bit of the venison. Will you have it? "

" No, thank you, man," answered Robin.

" Here 's a comb of honey as yellow as the gold in a lord's purse. Will you have it? "

" I can eat no honey," said Robin.

" Here are strawberries, and they were gathered with the dew of the morning on them. Will you take them, Master? "

" I will have no strawberries."

" Here 's white bread, and only yesterday it was baked in the bishop's oven. Will you taste it? " Robin shook his head. Then said William Scarlet : —

" Did you have bad dreams, Master? "

Robin Hood: His Book

"Bad dreams hide under roofs; they never come under the open sky."

"Then you are sick," declared William Scarlet, "and you must be bled."

So William Scarlet and Much the miller's son, and Arthur à Bland laid Robin gently down on the soft green moss. They bled him and they bled him.

"Do you feel any better, Master?" asked Arthur.

"No whit better do I feel," groaned Robin.

"It 's the witches that have hold of him," said Arthur, and the tears began to drop from his eyes like rain. "When the witches get into a man, you have to beat them out with oaken sticks, or else he 'll go mad."

They both cut stout oaken sticks to beat the witches out of Robin, and so well did they succeed that at the first blow he opened his eyes and said, "I feel better." At the second he sat up and said, "I 'm gaining fast," and at the third he stood up on his feet and said, "I feel well."

Then all the merrymen jumped for joy, and William Scarlet asked anxiously: —

"But, Master, was it the witches, think you?"

Robin Hood: His Book

" There 's no telling," answered Robin. " Mayhap it 's the wearisome life I 've led. It 's fourteen long days since I 've had a bit of sport. A man that 's been sick needs a change, and I 'll take a little journey for the good of my health I 'll go through the forest and see what I can see."

So Robin caught up his bow and arrows and bade farewell to his merrymen all. Through the forest he went, but never a bit of sport did he find. He walked along the path slowly and gloomily. His hunting cloak trailed in the dust, and his head hung down. He came to a wide brook, and over the brook lay a long plank. Robin put one foot on the plank just as some one else put one foot on the other end. The sun was in Robin's eyes, so he could not see who it was, but the shadow of the stranger was so long that it stretched away across the water, and in a minute a loud voice called : —

" Stand back and clear the bridge."

" Stand back yourself," shouted Robin ; but his voice trembled just a wee bit, for he was not really sure that it was a man ; he thought it might be the witches again.

" I 'll stand back after I 've crossed the bridge," said the voice. " Make way for your betters."

" I 'll make way for my betters when I find them," cried Robin. Just then the sun sank below the hill, and Robin saw at the other end of the bridge a man full seven feet tall, with fists like sledge-hammers and a staff like the mast of a vessel.

" It 's only a man," said Robin to himself, and he took another step forward and cried boldly : —

" Get you gone from the narrow bridge, or I 'll show you the way we do it in Bernisdale ;" and Robin drew from his quiver a broad arrow winged with a gray goose-quill.

" If you touch the string," cried the stranger, " over into the water you 'll go."

" I thought you might be witchcraft, but you 're only a simpleton," said Robin, "for I could send my good arrow clear and clear through you before you could strike a blow."

" If I 'm a simpleton, you 're a coward, that 's what you are," retorted the giant. " You have a bow, and I 've nothing but a staff."

" If that 's a staff, I wonder what a tree-trunk

Where are you now my fine fellow! cried John Little.

would be," thought Robin, but he called aloud : —

"Don't you move hand or foot, and I 'll go to the thicket and cut me a stick, and we 'll see who 's the better man."

Soon Robin came back, and then such a flourishing of staffs as there was just in the middle of the narrow bridge! The stranger struck the first blow, and the dust flew out of Robin's hunting-cloak till you could n't have seen the sun if it had been above the hill. Then Robin struck so hard that the bones of the stranger rang, until all the little birds drew their heads out from under their wings and began to sing. Then they struck at each other's head, and they were both so hot-headed that you could see fire at every stroke. At last the giant pushed Robin into the brook.

"Where are you now, my fine fellow?" he cried.

> "I 'm sailing happily down the flood
> And floating along with the tide,"

trolled Robin. "You 're a brave man, and you 've won the fight. Now I 'll give you the merriest time that you ever had in all your life."

Robin pulled himself out by a thorn-tree and shook the water from his buglehorn. Then he blew such a blast that the leaves on the trees began to fall because they thought a November gale was blowing.

In the wink of an eye there was a great rustling in the woods, and from east and west and north and south came Robin's good bowmen all dressed in Lincoln green. There were nine and sixty of them, and they all rushed up to Robin.

"Where have you been?" they cried, "and how came you so wet?"

"It's the laddie that's just crossed the plank," answered Robin. "He tumbled me into the stream."

"Then into the stream he goes himself," said Will Stutely.

"Nay, nay, hold!" cried Robin. "The man that I love best is the one that's gotten the better of me in a fair fight. I'll have no man to serve me that cannot beat me." Then said he to the stranger: —

"Will you be one of my bowmen and wear my livery, and learn to use the bow, and eat venison like a king's son, and have two new suits every year, and live in the good greenwood as free as the bird on the bough?"

"That will I, in faith, and right heartily, and here's my hand on it," said the stranger, and he squeezed Robin's hand till you could hear the bones squeak.

"What is your name?" asked Robin.

"John Little," replied the stranger. At this the whole nine and sixty bowmen burst out a-laughing.

"You shouldn't laugh at a bashful stranger lad like me," said John Little; "but I don't bear malice, and I'll shake hands with every one of you to prove it."

"He'll shake hands with us," murmured the nine and sixty; and each one of them put his right hand behind him.

Then William Scarlet stepped forward and said:—

"When a babe like this wee bit laddie comes, he must be christened. Who will give him a name?"

"I will," said Arthur à Bland. "We'll call him Little John."

Robin Hood: His Book

"What do they do at a christening?" asked William Stutely.

"They give the baby a gown," answered Much the miller's son.

"I'll give him the gown," declared Robin, "and it shall be of the Lincoln green, and I'll give him a bow, and a quiver full of arrows all winged with a gray goose-quill."

"Don't they do anything else at a christening?" asked William Stutely.

"Yes," answered Robin. "They have a feast."

"A feast, a feast," murmured the nine and sixty good bowmen; and they all set to and made ready for the christening feast. They had silver dishes from the sheriff's house, and golden dishes from the bishop's house, and venison from the king's forest, and they had honey and white bread, and wine and ale and beer, and fish and fowl, and roast and baked and broiled, and they ate and they drank, and they danced and they sang, till the moon was high up over the treetops.

And so it was that John Little was christened Little John and became one of Robin Hood's men and went to live in the good greenwood.

IV

THE BIRTH OF ROBIN HOOD

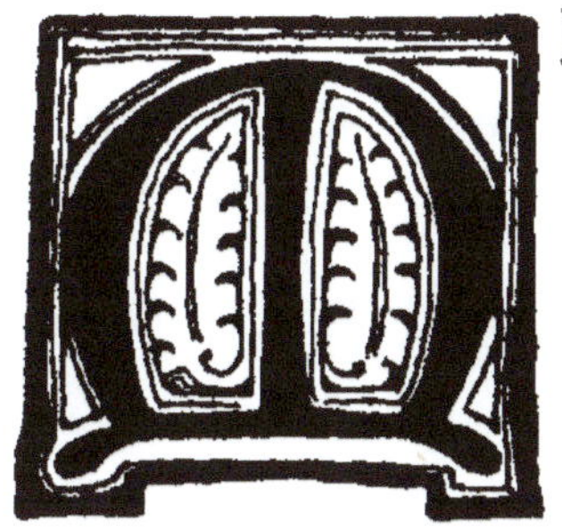ICKLE WILLIE had three good friends, and one day he went to them and asked:—

"Hughie and Jamie and Davie, will you tell me what a man must do when he would win a bonny maiden?"

"He must give her a gold ring and tell her that he loves her well," answered Hughie.

The next day, Mickle Willie went again to his three good friends and said:—

"I gave her the gold ring, and I told her that I loved her well, and all she would say was, 'There's many a man who has told me that,' and she would n't keep the ring. Jamie, what must a man do when he would win a bonny maiden?"

"He must steal her away by night," answered Jamie.

The next day Mickle Willie went again to his three good friends and said:—

"I went to the castle gate by night, and I knocked loud and long. When the lord came to me I said, 'I've come to steal away your daughter,' and he only laughed at me and shut the gate. Davie, what must a man do when he would win a bonny maiden?"

"He must tell her that he can't live without her," answered Davie.

So Mickle Willie went again to the bonny maiden and said:—

"Bonny maiden, I cannot live without you." But the maiden only answered:—

"You're living without me now, are you not?" Then she and her bower women drew the curtain tight. Mickle Willie went down the long hill to the meadow, and all the way he could hear the laughing of the lady and her bower maidens. He did not go back to his friends this time, but he went to the Way-off Tree; and there he thought and thought and thought. The sun came up on the left and went down on the right; and just as the moon rose, Mickle Willie jumped up and said:—

Robin Hood: His Book

" Three heads may be better than one when three would win a bonny maiden; but one head is better than three when it's one that would win her. I 'll use my own wits, and I 'll try to win the bonny maiden all by my lone self."

Off he set for the castle. He pounded on the gate till it trembled and shook, and he shouted in so great a voice that the banner on the tower began to wave in the moonlight : —

" Bonny maiden, bonny maiden, will you come down to the gate and speak with me ? "

Earl Richard heard the shouting, and he said to the bonny maiden : —

" That's Mickle Willie. Go you down to the castle gate and speak to him. See that you speak to him fairly and well, for now I bethink me, he's a mighty man, and if he 'll serve me, he 'll make a better squire than I 've had this many a day."

" It's not to win my father a squire that I 'll go," murmured the bonny maiden to herself, as she went slowly down the winding stair; and she asked of Mickle Willie : —

" Why do you come in the night and wake us from our sleep when the moon shines on the castle wall? The men that would serve **my** father come to us by daylight."

"It's not to serve your father that I'm come," said Mickle Willie, "it's to see your own self."

"But I've no wish to see you," retorted the bonny maiden.

"Say true, lassie, say true," whispered the old nurse who stood on the stair behind her.

Then said Mickle Willie: —

"They say that sometimes a maiden is wiser than Hughie and Jamie and Davie, and I've only come to ask you a question that three wise men and a fool cannot answer."

"And what is the question?" queried the bonny maiden, coming one step farther down the winding stair.

"I'll not trouble you with it to-night. I'll just bide under the shelter of the wall, and in the morning when the moon shines no more on the castle, then I'll come and ask you the question."

"But what is the question?"

"Will you grant me your pardon if I ask it?"

"Yes, yes," cried the bonny maiden impatiently.

Then said Mickle Willie slowly: —

Robin Hood: His Book

"You've asked me once to tell the question; that's one. You've asked me twice; that's two. You've promised me your pardon; that's three; but maybe, after all, I'd better go and ask Hughie and Jamie and Davie whether to tell it."

"No, no, tell me what the question is. I'll not be angry, and I'll give you the answer true as true. What is it?"

"Three wise men and a fool could n't answer it, and this is what it is: How is a man to win the hand of a bonny maiden, and that is yourself?"

"Say true, lassie, say true," whispered the nurse. "You're fairly caught now, lassie."

The bonny lassie thought for seven long minutes. Then she said slowly:—

"The man that wins me must be a lord of high degree, of course, and there are three things that he must do. He must mind my father's sheep for seven years. He must build me a bower all shining with the yellow topaz and with pearls and emeralds; and at my father's own bidding he must carry over the castle wall and far away the thing that my father holds dearest. Now you have your answer. Are there any more questions, Mickle Willie?"

"No, bonny maiden. I 'll just lay me down by the castle wall and sleep, and in the morning I 'll go to Earl Richard and ask if I may be his man."

The morning came, and Mickle Willie went to Earl Richard and begged to enter his service. Glad enough was the earl to gain so mighty a follower.

"What can you do?" he asked.

"I can ask questions that three wise men cannot answer; and I can win an answer that three wise men cannot get," said Mickle Willie. The earl looked puzzled, then his face grew clear.

"Can you lift the great stone by the gate?" asked he.

"Surely, I can do it with one hand," replied Mickle Willie, as he lifted the stone and tossed it over the wall.

"Men used to go by wit," said the earl, "but now they go by brawn. I 'll take you for my squire, and I 'll pay you more than any other man in my service." So it was that Mickle Willie became the squire of Earl Richard, who was the father of the bonny maiden.

Six days he served the earl, and on the seventh he said : —

"You say well that men go by brawn, but there 's been no test of brawn in all the long time that I 've been in your service. Let us have a trial to-morrow, and see whether it 's you or your neighbors that have the stronger squire."

" And what shall be the test ? " asked the earl.

" Let each man choose a burden to carry to the top of the castle wall, and he who has carried the heaviest shall have the prize."

" So shall it be," declared the earl ; and he sent a herald to all the country round about, and invited the squires of all the lords to a contest.

When the people had come together, the herald cried : —

" Now let every squire choose a burden and bear it to the top of the castle wall. Then shall he who has borne the heaviest have a reward, as much gold as he can carry away in both his hands."

Every squire turned to gaze at the castle wall.

" My sword is enough for such a climb as that," said one, and he took nothing more.

" My own body in its mail is all I care to take," laughed another. A third caught up a little fagot of sticks and a fourth a small round stone.

Every man started except Mickle Willie alone, and he stood just behind the squire without moving hand or foot.

" Mickle Willie," said the earl, " why do you not take a burden and climb the castle wall? Are you not stronger than all the other squires of all the other lords? A poor squire are you to leave your lord with no one to strive for him."

" I 'll go if you bid me," returned Mickle Willie. " And shall I choose my own burden ? "

" Surely," replied the earl.   " Take whatever burden you will, even if it is the castle keep itself."

" I 'll do what my master bids me," said Mickle Willie, and he put his strong arm about the bonny maiden who stood in the castle door.

In a minute he was on top of the wall. In another minute he had wrapped his scarlet cloak about the maiden, and with her in his arms he had sprung to the ground as lightly as a feather. Away and away and away he went, across the field and through the forest.

Nobody in the castle knew just what had happened. The knights on the ground said the maiden was caught up into a red cloud, and the squires on the wall said a flame of fire had swept her from their sight; and before the squires had come down or the knights had gone through the gate, Mickle Willie and the bonny maiden were so far away in the good greenwood that, hunt as he might, no knight and no squire could find a trace of them.

Far away on the other side of the forest was Mickle Willie with the bonny maiden.

"Why have you brought me so far, far away?" asked the bonny maiden.

"I brought you to be my own true bride," answered Mickle Willie. "Did you not tell me that the way to win you was to carry over the castle wall, at your father's own bidding, the thing that he holds dearest?"

"Yes, truly," said the bonny maiden, "and that have you done; but it's not all. The man that wins me must be a lord of high degree, and you're but the son of a shepherd out on the plain."

"Not so," answered Mickle Willie, "for I was born a lord of high degree; but he who is the shepherd's son sits in the hall that should have been mine own."

"Still must you go back and serve my father and mind his sheep for seven years," said the bonny maiden.

"Oh, but it's much more than seven years that I minded your father's sheep when I was only a wee bit laddie and abode with the shepherd on the plain," answered Mickle Willie.

"Not yet will I be your bride," declared the bonny maiden. "If he who is the shepherd's son sits in the hall that should have been your own, then surely you cannot give me a bower that shines with the yellow topaz and with pearls and emeralds."

"Can I not?" cried Mickle Willie happily. "Come, bonny maiden, see what I have for you." He took her by the hand, and through the wood they went like two children a-maying.

By and by they came to a bower that was fit for a queen. It was all of the green oak leaves, and the sun shone down among them. Around it grew tall white lilies, and when the bonny maiden came near, they bent low to kiss her white fingers.

Then the strong man, Mickle Willie, bowed himself before her and whispered softly: —

"Are not the lilies fairer than pearls? Are not the green oak leaves richer than emeralds? Does not the yellow sunshine glow clearer than the topaz? Here is even more than you asked, for does not the little brook sparkle more brightly than any diamond? And now, bonny maiden, will you not be my own true bride?"

The little bird on the tree overhead heard her answer. Mickle Willie had won the bonny maiden.

"Shall we go to the hall that ought to be mine own and cast out him that is the shepherd's son?" asked Mickle Willie. The bonny bride looked once more at the lilies and the oak leaves and the sunshine and the brook, and she answered: —

"Let us stay here together in the good greenwood, and leave the hall to him who is the shepherd's son." So Mickle Willie and his own true bride lived in the lily bower by the brook for a year and a day.

It came to pass that Earl Richard was wandering through the wood one morning, when he heard a low, sweet sound of music.

"It sounds like the song my daughter used to

sing," said the earl to himself. He pushed on softly, and soon he came to the oak-leaf bower. There sat the bonny bride, and on her knee was her fair young son.

" Are you a nymph of the wood or are you my own daughter ? " cried the earl.

" I 'm your own child," answered the bonny maiden. " Here is your grandson, and here is Mickle Willie, his father. Do you not remember that you told me yourself to speak to Mickle Willie fairly and well, that he might come and stay with us ? "

Straight into the diamond brook gazed the earl while one might have counted a score. The brook flashed and sparkled, and something sparkled in the eyes of the earl.

" I 'll grant you both pardon for the sake of the fair young child," said he. " And now come you three to the castle. The babe shall have his christening, and by and by I will give him all that is mine."

" I doubt me if he will stay in the castle," said Mickle Willie. " The babe that 's born among the lilies cannot abide within walls of stone."

Robin Hood: His Book

"Then every year when the leaves are green and the lilies blow, he shall come to the greenwood and live for a whole month in the oak-leaf bower," promised Earl Richard, "and when he is grown, he shall do as he will."

Then the babe that was born among the lilies was carried to the church and christened, and the name that was given him was Robin Hood.

Hughie and Jamie and Davie were all invited to the christening feast, and when they bade the merry company good-night, Hughie said to Mickle Willie: —

"Did I not tell you how to win her?"

"Did I not tell you how to win her?" asked Jamie.

"Did I not tell you how to win her?" asked Davie, and Mickle Willie answered: —

"Indeed, I thank you heartily for all the wise words that you gave me; and when my fair bride wearies of me and I weary of her, then will I come again to my three good friends to learn how to win the heart of a bonny maiden."

V

LITTLE JOHN LEARNS A TRADE

ASTER," said Little John, "I'm thinking of learning a trade."

"And what set you to thinking of that?" asked Robin.

"A man must fend for his old age," answered Little John thoughtfully. "If so be that the sheriff catches me, I'll have no old age; but it might be that the king would pardon me, and he'd not give me my bed and board as the sheriff would. I'd even have to look out for my own bread and my ale."

"And what'll be your trade?" asked Much the miller's son.

"Indeed, I'm not yet knowing."

"Will you be a butcher?" asked William Scarlet.

"A butcher sometimes sells good meat, and sometimes he sells poor," said Little John thoughtfully. "No, I'll not be a butcher."

"Will you be a baker?"

"No, Friar Tuck, I'll not be a baker. Sometimes the baker's loaf is full weight, and sometimes it's not. I would fain be honest."

" And will you be a candlestick-maker ? "

"No, Much the miller's son. My own father bought a candlestick once. It took his whole three-days' wages, and when he had it, it wasn't good metal, and it bent in the using. I'll not be a candlestick-maker."

"I'd be loath indeed to have one of my good men turn rogue," said Robin, "but, truly, I fear me there's no trade that's honest save our own."

"What think you of begging, Master Robin?" asked William Scarlet.

" A beggar has naught to do with poor meat," declared Robin thoughtfully. "He sells no light loaves, and he puts no poor metal into candlesticks. Begging is not a bad trade, my Little John."

"Indeed, I think I'll be a beggar, Master Robin. So will you give me a little bag for the bread, and a big bag for the cheese, and a bigger one than either for the gold that I 'll get."

Then the men put upon Little John a long gray cloak. It had more holes than there are leaves on the trees, and there was a patch of a different color for every different hole. They found him a hat, and that, too, had many holes, a different hole for every wind that blows. They brought him a stout oak-tree staff, and so he was made ready to go a-begging.

Then sang Little John: —

> " And a-begging I will go,
> And a-begging I will go ;
> With hat and cloak
> And staff of oak,
> A-begging I will go."

They all took hands and danced around a great tree and sang Little John's song together merrily. Then said Little John : —

" A good workman sets out for his work early in the morning, and I 'd best be on my road to the king's highway."

They went with him to the border of the forest, and there they said their farewells.

"See that you come back to us a master beggar," called Friar Tuck.

"We'll tie up our bags when we see you coming," said William Scarlet.

"Fare you well," cried Little John, waving the gray cloak and swinging the hat from the point of the staff; and away he went, singing : —

> "With hat and cloak
> And staff of oak,
> A-begging I will go."

"Hist!" said he to himself. "There be three master beggars, or I'm no bowman." He stood by the side of the road and waited for them to come along. One was blind, and one was deaf and dumb, and one was lame.

"That's just the company for me," thought Little John. He went up to them with his hat in his hand and said meekly : —

"Gentle sirs, would you let me join your noble company?"

"Who are you?" asked he that was lame.

"I'm only a country laddie, but I'd like well to learn a trade and bide with the great folk that journey about the land."

“ And what trade will you have ? ” asked he that was blind.

“ I ’d like to be a beggar,” answered Little John.

“ That ’s no easy trade to learn,” declared he that was lame. “ You ’d far better be the lord high chancellor.”

“ But the king ’s not asked me to be that,” said Little John.

“ Neither have we asked you to be a beggar,” retorted he that was blind, “ and what ’s more, I don’t like your looks.”

“ And you ’ve not the voice for a beggar,” said he that was deaf.

“ Stand there by the tree,” bade he that was blind, “ till we talk a bit by ourselves.”

They went a little way up the road, where they were out of Little John’s hearing.

“ He ’s a big, strong fellow,” whispered one, “and we ’d make him carry the bags.”

“ Those big fellows are always slow,” muttered another, “ and if the sheriff is after us, he ’ll soon catch the country boy, and his betters will get free.”

“ I say let ’s take him,” said the third.

Then they went back to Little John, who stood waiting meekly by the tree.

"We'll let you go along with us," declared one, "but you're only a 'prentice, and you're to carry the bags, and to have no part or lot in our gains for a year. There's much to learn in begging."

"Thank you humbly," quoth little John. "I'll bear the bags and willingly, for I would fain have an honest trade." So they put on him the bags for bread and the bags for cheese.

"Shall we give him the bags for gold?" whispered one.

"Why not?" whispered another. "They're heavy, and he's too stupid to make way with them." So the bags for gold were put on him.

"He shall walk a bit ahead of us," said he that was blind, "and then we can see if he thinks of running away."

"There's not another man in York that can run as fast as I," boasted he that was lame, "and I'd soon catch him if he tried any such tricks."

They had gone scarcely a mile down the highway when Little John turned back to his new masters in great excitement.

Robin Hood: His Book

" Master Beggars, Master Beggars," he cried,
" there be some rich men coming up the road.
One of them is the proud bishop. What do you
do first when you beg from a bishop ? "

The three beggars slipped into the hedge and
pulled their apprentice in after them.

" How many men are with him ? " asked he
that was dumb.

" Five, and well armed," answered he that was
blind.

" That 's none at all," whispered Little John
eagerly. " Shall I go out and beg? I have my
bow and arrows and a good stout staff."

" The fellow 's a fool," growled angrily he that
was lame. " Get in here, you country bumpkin,
and don't you stir finger or toe till they 're out
of sight."

Little John was sorely puzzled, but he said to
himself, " A 'prentice must mind his master," so
he lay still and asked no questions, and the proud
bishop went on his way.

The beggars had gone scarcely a mile farther
down the highway when Little John turned back
in greater excitement than before.

" Master Beggars, Master Beggars," cried he,

" here 's surely the one to beg of. He has hanged many a man on the gallows-tree but to get his gold and gear. He lives in a great stone house,

and with him be three knaves who 've many a time followed out good men and true to the very death. Will you not let me beg of him, Masters? My arrows go true, indeed they do, and it 's almost sure I am that he 'll give to us, for 't is but last month —" Then Little John remembered that he was no longer a bowman of the forest, but a 'prentice lad learning a trade, and he said not another word, even when the three beggars pulled him farther into the hedge than before.

"You've not the sense of a jack o' lantern," said they. "Would you beg of a man with three strong men to stand by him?"

"No, Masters, not if you tell me not," answered Little John humbly, "but I'm almost sure he'd have given me something. He always —"

"It's near nightfall," said he that was deaf and dumb, "and by the border of the forest there's a place where we can get our supper. Mayhap we'll get more. When a house is made larger, there's many a time more in it."

They went on till they came to a little cottage with one old room and one new one. There was a cheery fire in the tiny fireplace, and sitting at her wheel was a merry little old woman singing:—

> "Monday I wash and Tuesday I iron,
> Wednesday I cook and I mend;
> Thursday I brew and Friday I sweep,
> And baking day brings the end."

"I'll keep back a bit," thought Little John, "for it's she that saved the life of Master Robin, and I'd not have her know I'm but a 'prentice. I'll be a master beggar first." So he said to the three beggars: —

"It's no supper that I care for to-night. I'll just lay me down under the window and rest. My feet are weary from walking on the highway."

Little John lay down, and the three beggars pushed open the door. The merry little old woman gave a little scream, then she curtseyed and said timidly: —

"I'm but a little old woman, sirs, and is there aught that I can do for great folk like you?"

"Get us some supper," bade he that was dumb, "and see to it that you put on the best there is in the house."

"Yes, Masters," said the little old woman; and she hurried to stir up the fire and set an oaten cake to baking on the hearth.

"Cook some eggs," bade he that was blind.

"Yes, Masters," said the little old woman, "but, indeed, I have only two; the hen did not lay to-day."

"Get another, or it will be the worse for you," cried he that was blind.

"What's that?" said Little John to himself, and then he thought, "May be it's only their way, and they'll give her a broad goldpiece and wish her well when they go;" so he said nothing, but he kept watch through the window.

The three beggars sat down at the table and ate and ate and ate.

"Surely the merry little old woman will have naught to eat to-morrow," thought Little John, "but the goldpiece will buy her something;" so he lay still and kept his eyes open and said nothing.

When the beggars had eaten all that they could eat, he that was dumb said: —

"What have you in the other room? Folk don't build rooms when they've naught to put into them. Bring it out to us."

"Truly, Masters, it was good friends that gave me the room," answered the little old woman.

"Bring out what's in it — or stop, I'll see for myself;" and he that was lame pushed open the door and brought out a roll of cloth of blue, and

an armful of silken kerchiefs and shoes and stock·
ings, and warm blankets for the bed.

"Pile them up and make a good bundle of
them," bade he that was lame, "and the country
lad outside shall carry it."

"It 'll take a whole handful of goldpieces to pay
for that," thought Little John; and still he kept
his eyes open and said nothing.

As soon as the men had tied up the bundle, two
of them carried it out of the door and called:—

"Here, you country fellow, come and take the
bundle."

"But you 've not paid the little old woman,"
said Little John in surprise, "and she 's in the
corner by the spinning-wheel, and she 's crying."

"What 's that to you? You 're to learn the
trade, are n't you?" demanded he that was
blind.

"This is no honest trade," shouted Little John;
and with his stout oaken staff he laid about him
so lustily that the three beggars all ran for their
lives, and he that was lame ran fastest of all.

Little John went in and comforted the frightened little old woman until she was merry again.
He carried back the great bundle, he put a stronger

bolt on her door, and he gave her a bright new goldpiece from his belt. Then he went back to the forest, and as he walked down the lane, he could hear her singing cheerily: —

"And baking day brings the end."

"There 's one coming through the forest," said George à Green. "He wears a hat with a hole for every wind that blows, and a gray cloak with as many patches as there are leaves on the trees. Who might it be, Master?"

"Surely," said Robin, "it 's our own Little John. Little John," he called, "come and show us your skill. We 'll all come out in the moonlight, and do you see whether you can beg the gold out of our belts and the cloaks off our backs."

"I 'm not learning begging any more," said Little John.

"Have you been 'prentice and journeyman and master all in one day?" asked Friar Tuck.

Then Little John told them about his trying to learn the trade of begging, and his being forbidden to beg from either bishop or sheriff. "I 've not the skill to be a great man," said he. "I fear me

I 'd never learn to take from the poor and be afraid of the rich."

" But what are all the bags you 're carrying ? " asked Friar Tuck.

" There are my own that I started with," answered Little John, throwing the three empty bags on the ground, " and there are the three for the bread and the three for the cheese and the three for the gold."

" And what is in the three for the gold ? " asked William Scarlet.

" Indeed, I know not," said Little John. " I would have given the bags back, but my masters ran so fast that I doubt if I could have caught them."

" And what made them run ? " asked George à Green.

Then Little John finished his story and told about the beggars' attack on the merry little old woman. " And when they came out," said he, " they ran away so fast that I could do little for them."

" But what made them run ? " asked Friar Tuck.

" I don't know unless it was my stout oaken

staff," answered Little John. "Now I think of it, I did give them just a wee bit blow or two."

"Did he that was lame run away?" asked Robin.

"Yes, surely."

"Did he that was blind come to his eyesight?"

"Yes, surely."

"And he that was dumb, did he learn to speak?"

"Yes, surely, and louder than both the others."

"Oh, Master," cried Friar Tuck, "look at the gold in the bags!"

"Indeed, I would n't willingly have run away with their gold," said Little John.

"But you 've made the lame one walk, the dumb one speak, and the blind one see," declared Robin. "You 've learned to be a doctor of physic, and a doctor has ever his fee."

"A man never knows where his arrow will go," quoth Little John. "I must be full as stupid as they said, to be learning one trade when I thought I was learning another."

"I 've been thinking," said Robin the next morning, "that begging might be a good trade after all, and now that Little John has come out a doctor of physic, I 'm fain to go on the highway and see if a man may not be a beggar and yet be honest."

" But there 's many a man that 'll know your face, Master Robin," objected George à Green.

" Not when I 've the hood of a friar well drawn over it," replied Robin. "Come, my merrymen all, make me into a friar, and it 's out into the world I 'll go."

Then the men put upon Robin the coarse gray gown of a begging friar, and a girdle of rope and a rosary of wooden beads. He set out on his way, and when he came to the highway, he drew the gray hood down over his face so that even the sheriff would not have known him.

He took his stand by the side of the way, ready to beg from the first one that came along. Soon he saw a parish priest walking slowly and carrying a great bag. Robin could see that it was all the priest could do to keep the bag from rolling back down the hill.

"Good morrow," said Robin. "Would you have my help in getting the bundle up the hill?"

" I 'm grateful," answered the priest. " They 're

for the Widow Black. A kind gentleman gave me the bricks, and I can soon build her a good chimney with them. It is n't often that a priest has so fine a gift."

" I 'll carry them up the hill for you," said Robin, and he took up the heavy load. When he laid it down at the house of the widow, the priest said : —

" It 's little that a parish priest has to give, but I 've at least a roof over my head for the night, and I seldom have to fast save on the fast days. I can easily spare this silver groat for you who have neither bed nor board save what you can beg from day to day."

" Thank you kindly," said Robin. " I 'll not forget the good priest who gave me the silver groat. Mayhap I can do somewhat for you before the rain falls."

The priest went to work on the chimney as cheerily as if he had not just given away his dinner. As for Robin, he slipped out on a little crossroad and knocked at a cottage door.

" John à Mill," he called, "come out a bit." A stout working-man came to the door, and as Robin threw back his friar's hood, he cried : —

"It's Master Robin! Come in and sit by the fire and let the good wife make you a cake;" but Robin shook his head.

"Not to-day, my man. Will you do a bit of work for me?"

"Is there aught that I would not do for you, Master Robin?"

"You know how to lay bricks. Will you go a half-hour's walk above where the crossroad joins the highway, and when you see a parish priest trying to build a chimney, will you set to work and do it for him?"

"That will I do and aught else that's for you, Master Robin."

"Here's a goldpiece for you, and here's another for you to give to the priest. Tell him a friar sent it to him;" and Robin laughed to think how surprised the good man would be.

"Surely, begging may be an honest trade," thought Robin. "I took from the rich — and that's myself, and I gave to Widow Black — and she's the poor. That's honest. I'll try it again;" and again he took his stand by the highway.

Now came two monks riding on tall horses

that held their heads proudly at carrying so great men. The monks wore gowns of the finest cloth, fastened under the chin with golden clasps set with many bright stones. The sleeves of the gowns were trimmed with as rich fur as if the monks had been lords of high degree, and the little bells on their bridle reins jingled as loud as if they had been princes.

"They're the ones for me," thought Robin. He went up to them humbly and said: —

"Good monks, I 've been wandering all the day, and never a bit of bread have I had from goodman or goodwife, and never a bit of drink has any one put to my lips. For the sake of our Blessed Lady will you not cross my hand with a silver groat?"

"Never a groat have we," said one of the monks, and the other added: —

"It 's not many hours ago that we passed by Bernisdale. We were set upon by the rascally outlaw that they call Robin Hood, and he robbed us of every penny."

"And could one man rob two?" asked Robin.

"He caught us both by the foot as we sat on our horses, trying hard to get back to the convent for prayers, and when he had us on the ground, he took away every silver pound and every silver penny. I 've nothing left but this brass farthing."

" Should you know the outlaw if you saw him ? " asked Robin, throwing back his hood.

" Would not a man that 's been robbed know the man who 's robbed him ? " demanded the first monk.

" Monk or no monk, I 'd take him by the throat if I saw him," boasted the second.

" Here he is," cried Robin ; and the two monks galloped away as fast as they could go. Robin took a short cut across the fields, and when they came to the crossroads, there he stood in a bush. As they went by, he caught each one by the foot and pulled him down to the ground.

" A man should tell the truth himself," said he, " and it 's no more than right that he should help other men to tell the truth. I fear there 's no making honest men of you, but I 'll keep you from one lie, for, in faith, I 'll make good the story you told me this morning. Give me your money, every silver pound and every silver penny."

Robin Hood: His Book

" But, indeed, we 've no money," pleaded the
elder monk. " Let us go, good Robin. We
must be back before the convent bell rings for
prayers."

" We 'll have the prayers," said Robin, " but
it 'll be in the good greenwood." So he drove the
horses on ahead and took the two monks, leading
one by his right hand and one by his left, down
the forest road.

When they came to where the good bowmen
were, then said Robin : —

" This begging is not so bad, after all, but it 's
more comfortable to do it in a man's own home,
so I 've brought the two monks here to beg of
them. Now, sir monks, will you give a poor friar
some money for his dinner ? "

" We 've no money," persisted they.

" Then get you down on your knees," bade
Robin. " A monk without a penny 's in a hard
case, so call you upon every saint that you ever
heard of till you get some coins in your pockets."

There was nothing else for the monks to do,
so down on their knees they went, and " Send us
money," they cried to every saint that ever they
had heard of.

“ Louder,” bade Robin; and they cried louder, “ Send us money! send us money!”

“ Faster,” bade Robin; and they cried faster, “ Send us money! send us money!”

“ Wring your hands,” bade Robin; and the monks wrung their hands.

“ Weep,” commanded Robin; and they wept as well as they could. It was better done than one would have expected, for they were really frightened lest they should lose their money after all. They were still more frightened when Robin said: —

“ You ’ve done very well. You ’ve called on so many saints that some one among them has surely heard you; so now look you in your pockets, and see how many goldpieces you find.”

The monks put their hands into their pockets, and then they pulled them out.

“ There ’s never a goldpiece, and there ’s never a silverpiece,” they declared.

“ I ’ll have no such word as that said of the good saints,” cried Robin. “ In faith, you ’ll make my young men think the saints don’t hear you at all. Stand you close about, my merrymen, and I 'll show you plain and clear that when a good monk calls on the saints for money, he 's sure to get it."

Then while the bowmen stood about and laughed to hear the groans of the monks, Robin put his hand into the monks' pockets, and drew out one goldpiece after another until five hundred good broad pieces of red gold lay on the ground.

"Now I've made your story good," declared Robin. "I 've made you honest men in spite of yourselves, and one should give to honest men, so here 's fifty pounds apiece for you. Get on your horses and haste you back, or you 'll be late when the convent bell rings for prayers. And, Little John, I 'm not so sure as I might be that begging 's not as good as preaching. The preacher will mayhap keep the man from telling the false stories, but the beggar can make the stories come true."

As for the monks, they dared not speak a word, but they thought first one thing and then another thing.

VI

ROBIN HOOD AND THE GOLDEN ARROW

IT'S a fine thing to be a great man," said the sheriff of Nottingham, "but we have our troubles."

"I know you do," agreed the sheriff's wife. " There are those new clothes that came too late to wear to the Lord Mayor's feast, and I'm almost sure that the stone house to the west of us is going to be larger than ours. What's more, there's a wretched little old woman that lives in a thatched cottage by the forest, and she wears a cloak that's finer than mine. I know it is, for she had the boldness to walk into the church before me, and I felt of it when she was in the door. It came from over the seas, I know that; and it's a good twelve threads to the inch finer than mine. It's grand to be great folk, as you say, but even great folk have their worriments."

[75]

Robin Hood: His Book

"It's worse than a woman's cloak that worries me," said the sheriff. "It's the bold and sturdy thief that lives in the forest who's wearing my life away. He's robbed the monks, and he's robbed the bishop. I doubt not he'd rob even me if he got the chance; but I look out for him. It takes a wise man to catch me asleep."

"Indeed it does," agreed his wife.

"If the fine cloak's a trouble to you, what do you think it is to me, when I'm as sure as I want to be that it was the thief who gave it to the old woman? And that's worse than all his robbing of the bishop, and worse than his shooting of the king's deer, for he's giving fine clothes to poor folk, and he's putting new thatch on their roofs, and he's paying their rent for them and carrying them loads of wood when they ought to be out in the forest picking up sticks for themselves. They'll think they're as good as we great folk before long. I doubt not he's already given them white bread and wine instead of their oat cake and water."

"And can you not catch the thief?"

"No more than you could catch the wind. He's here and he's there, and if you get him into the prison, he 'll find a way out. The worst of it is, I fear the king 'll think I 'm not trying to catch him. I believe I 'll go to London and tell the king what a pest the fellow is, and ask what he thinks would be a good way to catch him."

"Well, now, I would n't do that," said the sheriff's wife. " I know that when Jane came to me and told me the butter would n't come, I just said, ' Jane, you 've got the churn, have n't you? And you 've got the dasher, have n't you, and the cream ? ' and when she said 'Yes,' I said to her, said I, ' Now you 've the churn and the dasher and the cream, and it 's your part to make the butter.' "

So said the sheriff's wife, but the sheriff thought : —

"My wife may talk, but I know well enough she was glad to know that Jane was trying to make the butter and was worried because it did n't come, and I think the king would be pleased to know that I 'm troubled about Robin Hood, and that I 'm not forgetting my business. There never was a man yet that did n't like other folk to ask him for counsel, and the king 's but a man for all his crown and his throne."

Robin Hood: His Book

The sheriff put on his best clothes and
mounted his horse and set out for London town.
All the way he was planning what he would say

to the king, and how faithful the king would
think him, when it was so plain that the loss of
even one single thief was such a trouble to him.

When he was admitted to the royal audience
chamber, the king listened to the story of the
sad deeds of the robber bold, of how he had

stolen from the monks and from the bishop, **and** how, if the great man before him had not been so very wise, the outlaw would have stolen from even the king's sheriff of Nottingham.

When the story was done, the king said: —

" My good servant, you have your full appointment as Lord High Sheriff of Nottingham, have you not?"

" Yes, my Lord King," answered the sheriff.

" And is there need of any new law against robbery?"

" No, my Lord King."

" Then you have come to London only to ask my advice concerning the man that troubles you?"

" Yes, my Lord King."

" That is well. Now the very best advice I can give you is to go home and catch him. My Lord Chamberlain, see you to it that the High Sheriff of Nottingham has proper refreshment and is shown all courtesy. When he would return to Nottingham, have him escorted to the city gate by four members of the Royal Troop."

The sheriff backed out of the audience-room, and the king whispered to the queen: —

Robin Hood: His Book

"Did n't I do that well now?"

The Lord High Sheriff was feasted, and then he was escorted to the city gate by four members of the Royal Troop. He was surely the happiest man that went out of London that day, and he thought he was the greatest until he reached home and told his wife about the king's graciousness to him. He told her about the feasting and the Royal Troop, and a proud woman was she; but when he repeated what the king said when he asked for advice, the sheriff's wife looked very grave.

"It is n't every man that is great enough to ask the king for advice," said he.

"It is n't every man that is fool enough," retorted the sheriff's wife.

"What!" cried the sheriff.

Then the sheriff's wife explained that in spite of the feasting and the Royal Troop, the king had not given him one word of advice, but had only made fun of him. "And now you must catch the outlaw," she said, "or another year I fear me we 'll have to leave the fine stone house, and another man will be the Lord High Sheriff of Nottingham."

The sheriff was thoroughly humbled and badly frightened.

"Whatever shall I do? Won't you help me?" he begged. "They say a woman's wit is keener than a man's. Can't you devise some trick to catch the thief? If you will plan a way to get him, I'll send to Flanders, and I'll buy you the finest cloak that's to be had for money."

"I'll think about it," she answered rather loftily, "and if my own wit gives out, why, I can go up to London and ask the king." The sheriff only groaned.

The next morning the sheriff's wife woke her husband at the first crowing of the cock.

"I've thought of something," she said, "and if you do exactly what I tell you and don't wander off into something that you think is just as good, you'll catch the bold outlaw."

The sheriff promised faithfully that he would do just as she bade, and she said:—

"Now who are the best archers in all the North Countree?"

"Why, Robin Hood and his men, of course," answered the sheriff.

"Did you ever know an archer that did n't want to show his skill?"

"No," said the sheriff, "but what has that to do with it?"

"Why, I should think a bat would see. Send criers through all the country round about and proclaim a shooting match. Offer a golden arrow or a silver bow, or a belt all set with shining stones, and you 'll see Robin and his men fast enough."

"But how 'll I know them?" asked the sheriff helplessly.

"I do believe you have n't waked up yet. If Robin and his men are the best shots, then keep fast hold of the best shots, and you 'll have Robin and his men."

The sheriff was delighted. "You are the wisest woman in Nottingham town," said he. "I 'll send for that cloak to-morrow; and when we 've caught Robin and he 's safe in the hands of the king, I 'll send to France and buy a satin gown, the best that can be found."

That very day the sheriff sent the criers through all the North Countree. They rang their bells, and they cried : —

Robin Hood: His Book

"O hear ye, O hear ye! A shooting match will be held on Nottingham Green, on midsummer day, in the afternoon. The Lord High Sheriff of Nottingham has offered for the prize an arrow with golden head and silver shaft. O hear ye, O hear ye!"

Of course the crier did not go into the forest, but there were people enough who were glad to tell the great news to Robin and his men.

"Make you ready, my merrymen all," bade he, "and we'll go to Nottingham and have some sport."

Then stepped forward a young man, one David of Doncaster, and said he:—

"Master Robin, let us stay in the good greenwood. This match is no good match and true; it is but a trick to beguile us archers into the hands of the sheriff. Be ruled by me this time, Master."

Robin was not pleased. "David of Doncaster," said he, "did I not know you for the brave man that you are, I should say that was the speech of a coward. How know you better than another man that the match is but a trick?"

Robin Hood: His Book

Now in the sheriff's house was a little serving-maid, and she it was that had told David; but this he could not tell, so he hung his head, and made no reply.

"I say let us go to the match," quoth Master Robin, "let what will come of it. Little John, what say you?"

"Let us go, Master," said Little John, "and if there 's a trick, we 'll meet it with another trick. We 'll wear no Lincoln green, but one shall put on white, another red, another yellow, and another blue. We 'll mix with the other men; no two of us shall stay together; and if among us we do not win the arrow with the golden head, we 're no true archers."

Then away they went from the greenwood to the shooting match on Nottingham Green. No two of them went together, and when they were mixed with the eight hundred men who were on the Green, it would have puzzled Robin himself to pick them out. It was no wonder that the sheriff could not find them.

"Oh, well," said he, "it will be easy enough when the shooting begins. I shall just watch for a little company that keep by themselves, and

Robin Hood: His Book

I 'll have my men ready to follow them." To be
sure, his wife had said, " Keep fast hold of the
best shots," but when he thought it over he said
to himself : —

" A woman knows naught about shooting. It 's
a man's business to understand such matters, and
I know well that a bowman 's not always sure
of making his very best shot. Even Robin and
his men may make a miss; but if I watch for
a little group of men that keep by themselves,
I 'll be sure of them."

The shooting began, but watch as he would,
the sheriff could see no little group of men that
kept by themselves, and were in any way different
from the rest of the eight hundred that were
trying for the golden arrow. One man and then
another shot.

" Good for the brown ! "
" Blue jacket, blue jacket ! "
" Yellow forever ! "
" Green 's the color ! "
" Cheer for the white, the white ! "
" The red has it, the red, the red ! "

So the crowd shouted. It was the man in red
that made the best shot, and he it was who was

called up before the sheriff to receive the arrow with the golden head and the silver shaft.

Now Robin was the man in red, and he and his men went home to the greenwood, not all together, of course, but each one took a different road, and went with a group of bowmen from some other part of the North Countree. At last they met on the edge of the forest. They were all merry and light of heart save Robin, and he, even with the golden-headed arrow stuck into his belt, looked sorry and vexed.

"What is it, Master Robin?" asked Little John. "You have won the prize, and it was the proud sheriff himself who gave it to you and told you that the whole North Countree was proud of you, and that you were an honor to every man that ever bent a bow. What more can you ask? He never guessed it was you."

"That is what grieves me," said Robin sadly. "The proud sheriff will never know that it was I to whom he gave the golden arrow. I'd willingly give the arrow back to him, and a hundred marks with it, if there was only some way of letting him know to whom he made his fine speech."

Robin Hood: His Book

"Master," said Little John, "you took my advice before and you found it good. Will you take it once more?"

"Speak on," bade Robin, "speak on. Your wit is as quick as a woman's. If the proud sheriff had but borrowed a woman's wit to help him, he'd have put me in the lowest dungeon cell before now."

"Let us write him a letter, Master, and tell him who it was that bore away his golden arrow. Friar Tuck can pen it."

"But how'll we send it?" objected Robin. "No one of my men shall risk his life to carry such a letter as that."

"Trust me once more, Master," said Little John. "I'll go nowhere near the reach of the proud sheriff, but yet he shall have the letter before nightfall."

When the match was over, the sheriff had to stay a long time on the green, for there were so many people who wished to tell him what a beautiful prize he had given and what a successful day it had been. At last he started for home. His wife had gone as soon as the shooting was over, and she had made ready the finest dinner that could be imagined. As the sheriff came up the steps, she met him in the doorway, as smiling as two May mornings.

"I've been thinking," she said, "that we'd take the thousand marks' reward that the king offered and make the house as big as the one to the west of us, and mayhap a little bigger. Which cell did you put him in?"

"Put whom in?" demanded the sheriff a little shortly.

"Robin, of course, the man in red that made the best shots of all."

"That was n't Robin," declared the sheriff. "Robin was n't there. I watched for him every minute."

The sheriff's wife had for a moment nothing to say, — a thing that did not often happen. While she stood staring into her husband's face, a boy came to the steps.

"Here be an arrow, and there's somewhat tied to it," said he. "It was shot over the wall, and the priest said it was for you, and you'd mayhap give me a silver penny for bringing it."

The sheriff took the arrow and handed the

boy a silver penny. Tied to the arrow was a bit of parchment, and the sheriff read:—

"This arrow is from Robin Hood, in return for the golden one that the sheriff courteously bestowed upon him to-day."

"What are you waiting for?" growled the sheriff, for the boy was still hanging curiously about. The boy went away, but the sheriff was soon sorry that he had gone, for when the two were alone, the sheriff's wife had something to say.

<h1 style="text-align:center">VII</h1>

ROBIN AND THE TINKER

T was on the way to Nottingham town that Robin met a
merry young man stepping
nimbly along and singing at
the top of his voice:—

> " From Banbury I come,
> And a tinker lad am I.
> I 'll mend your kettles, pots, and pans,
> Oh, call as I pass by."

" Hallo ! " called Robin.

"Yes, sir. Pot or pan or kettle, sir? Mend
it before you can say ' Robin Hood,' sir. Where
is it, sir ? "

" Why, I have n't any pots or pans or kettles,"
answered Robin Hood, with a look of surprise.
" I just called because you asked me to. Why
should I have a kettle ? "

"To cook your dinner," said the jolly tinker. " You had a dinner yesterday, had you not ? "

" To be sure."

" And you 'll have one to-day ? "

" Mayhap."

" Then mayhap you 'll need a kettle mended to cook it in."

" I 've no thought of kettles," said Robin, making a long face. " There 's sad news abroad."

" And what might it be ? " asked the tinker.

" Two men of your own craft were set in the stocks."

" And wherefore ? "

" For singing on the highway, or else it was for drinking too much ale and beer, I forget which. What news have you ? "

"Oh," said the jolly tinker, "indeed there 's no news at all, and in faith I fear there 'll not be till the outlaw 's caught."

" Who is the outlaw, and what will they do when they catch him ? "

" You must live in a molehill not to know that the land 's alive with men who want to get the king's reward. He 's offered a thousand marks to the one that 'll bring Robin Hood to him alive and unhurt. No one knows what the king will do with him, but they say he 'll make a prison that 's stronger than ever prison was before, and that when he once gets him safely in it, he 'll build a gallows, and it 'll be higher than ever gallows was before, and he 'll hang the outlaw with a stronger rope than ever man was hanged with before."

"And does it make a man any better to hang him?"

"Oh, well, there are plenty of men, but work 's not easy to find, and the king will pay well for the prison-building and the gallows-building and the rope-making. And Jack Ketch himself, why, there are so many thieves and sturdy beggars in the kingdom that Jack is getting rich as a lord on hanging them. I 'd not wonder if they made him a lord some day. It 's an easy life he has of it."

"Yes, hanging is almost as easy as being hanged," said Robin thoughtfully. "Indeed, I 'd not know which of the two trades to choose. A man must need a long time of 'prenticeship before he can ply either of them with a good heart."

Robin Hood: His Book

"See here," said the jolly tinker. "Suppose we go shares. I have a warrant —

> " From Banbury I come,
>   And a tinker lad am I ;
>   I 'll mend your kettles, pots, and pans,
>   Oh, call as I pass by."

So sang the tinker, stopping short in his offer to Robin, for they were passing by a little group of houses. No one came out to accept the tinker's invitation, and he went on :—

" It 's only right for a man to make an honest penny when he can, and I 've a good strong warrant from the sheriff to take Robin Hood if I come across him in my roamings. It may as well be myself as another man that 'll get the thousand marks."

" They say that Robin has a way of slipping out of the very hands of the man that thinks he has him," said the tinker's companion.

" He won't slip out of mine," declared the tinker stoutly. " When I 've given him one blow with my soldering iron — and I 'll not strike any harder than I must, for the king won't have him hurt — I 'll just put this little brass kettle over his head, and I 'll tie his hands, and I 'll

Robin Hood: His Book

lead him up to the king's palace, and I'll **say,**
'Sir King, here's the man you want.' Then the
king will say, 'Thank you, young tinker from
Banbury. Here's the thousand marks, and here's
a hundred more, because you brought him here
to my own gate yourself.' Then I'll have a man
to go about with me and carry the irons, and I'll
have a fine blue cloak, and I'll no longer eat my
dinner from a bag under a hedge, but I'll go
straight up to the front door of the inn, and I'll
say, 'Dinner for a traveller. Look to it now, and
see that you make no delays. A man who has
weighty business on hand can't be hindered by
cooks and scullions.'"

"My, but won't that be fine!" exclaimed
Robin, looking with wide-open eyes into the
tinker's face.

"That's just what it will be," declared the
tinker. "And now I've somewhat to say to you,"
he went on. "You live hereabouts, don't you?"

"Yes."

"Now I don't know this part of the land so
well as I do some others, and I'll make you an
offer. I'm not greedy, I'm not, and if you'll help
me find Robin Hood, I'll give you half the

money. You don't look dull, and if you're with a man of wit awhile, it'll do wonders for you. I'll just take you about with me to carry the bag and the irons and the solder, and when we get the king's reward, I'll give you a full half of it. I'll even give you half of the hundred marks that he'll give me over and above the reward. What do you say? It isn't every man that gets a chance like that."

"No, it's not," said Robin gravely. "Are you sure that the warrant is all right? You know you might lose all the reward if you took a man without a true warrant. Will you let me have a glance at it? If it's all right, I'd not wonder if I could give you a look at the fellow this very night. I'll not promise that you can catch him, or that you can hold him if you do catch him, for they say he's as slippery as three eels in a bunch. I'd not like to risk my neck in anything unlawful. Have you the warrant with you?"

"To be sure I have," answered the tinker. "I paid a good price for it, too, and I'll trust no man to take it into his hands. It'll sometimes do well enough for other men to nap, but a tinker must keep his eyes open. A kettle that looks well may have a hole in it."

"Very likely you 're right," said Robin. "You 're a stranger in these parts, you say, and I might even be one of Robin Hood's own men for all you could tell."

"Not you," laughed the tinker; "you 're not big enough. I 've heard too many stories of Robin and his men to fear you. Why, man, they say that if one of those fellows is in prison, two or, at the most, three of them will come up to the door and call out, 'Give us our man,' and if the jailer says no, they strike just one blow on the door, and the door falls in. Then they all walk off together as gay as princes."

"They must be strong indeed," agreed Robin simply. "Maybe the one that I thought was Robin was n't the real Robin at all. A man often makes a mistake."

"Mistake or no mistake, I 'll take you," said the jolly tinker. "Only if you 're going along with me, see to it that you keep your eyes open. It won't do for a tinker or a tinker's man to be napping. You 'll slip by a hole every time you do it."

Robin Hood: His Book

Robin swung the bag over his shoulder, and on they went together along the road to Nottingham. The tinker had a stout staff, and Robin had a sword, so there was no fear of robbers, and both the tinker and his man had a pleasant walk.

When they came near to Nottingham town, the tinker said:—

" Now, my man, we 'll sit down here under the hedge and eat our bread and cheese. When we 've the king's reward, we 'll go to the tavern like the great folk, and call for wine and baked fowl; but to-day it 's bread and cheese or it 's nothing. You shall have your full share, even if you have done no work as yet. I 'm not the one to pinch a man in his victuals."

" There 's something else we might do," suggested Robin. " I 've one piece of gold in my belt, and if we 're to get the king's reward so soon, there 's no use in saving it. Let 's go to the tavern as if we were great folk already and have our wine and baked fowl."

" You 're a free-handed fellow," said the tinker. " We 'll go if you say so, and I 'll tell you one thing, no man loses aught by treating me handsomely. The man that mends a hole for me never fails of his pay."

To the inn they went. Robin gave the orders, and he ordered not only wine and ale and beer and baked fowl, but many other things. There was soon such a dinner on the table as the tinker had never seen before.

" And are you sure the goldpiece will pay for it all? " he whispered a little anxiously.

" Sure as sunrise," declared Robin. " I 've been at the inn before. I 've not always carried a tinker's bag."

The tinker's mind was at rest. He ate and he ate and he ate, as never man ate before. Then he drank and he drank and he drank, as never man drank before. He was the happiest tinker in all Yorkshire. At last he fell asleep, and then he was the happiest tinker in all dreamland.

When he was once sound asleep, Robin reached softly into his bosom and took out the warrant.

" A man that would travel should n't be loaded down with too much baggage," said he thoughtfully. " It would be only kindness to free the good tinker from the burden," so he slipped the

Robin reached softly into his bosom and took out the Warrant.

warrant gently into the open fire. Then he beckoned to the landlord:—

"My friend," said he, "this man is to pay the scot, and if he thinks it ought to come from my own leathern belt, you can tell him where to look for me."

"Surely, Master Robin," whispered the host, with a wide grin. "But, sir, have you been well served? Is there aught I can do for you?"

"Nothing, my friend," whispered Robin. "When I come back to-night — and it 'll be in good time — just have a fine supper ready for us, will you, the very best there is in the house?"

"For two?" asked the landlord.

"Yes," answered Robin, "for me and the good man that dined with me. Farewell," and away he went to the forest.

When the tinker awoke, he was as dazed a man as there was in Nottingham. He rubbed his eyes and looked about him. He was in an inn, there was no doubt of that. The table was before him, and it was spread with the remains of the feast.

"I 've certainly had my dinner," said the tinker to himself, "have n't I?" and he felt to see if his belt was tight. "Yes, I 've had my dinner."

The landlord had been watching, and now he came up to the tinker with outstretched hand.

"Ten shillings for the dinner, please you," said he.

"Ten shillings!" cried the tinker. "I never ate a dinner in my life that cost more than fourpence. Ten shillings! Why, that 's more than I can save in half a year. And I 'll need it, too, to pay my way up to London when I carry the outlaw to the king."

"And who might the outlaw be?" asked the landlord, with a sly wink to his wife, who stood at his right hand.

"Robin Hood, of course," replied the tinker. "I 've a warrant for him, and I 'm going to catch him and take him to the king to get the reward. Here 's the warrant."

The tinker put his hand into his bosom, but no warrant was there.

"Oh, woe 's me, woe 's me," he cried. "And I paid a whole shilling to have it all written out. It said I might take the outlaw wherever I could find him."

"You found him fast enough," said the landlord,

with another wink to his wife. "Why did n't you take him to the king?"

"What mean you?" cried the tinker, starting up so suddenly that the landlady spread her arms over the cups and the trenchers, lest the table should be overthrown.

"Did n't you know that the good friend who dined with you was Robin himself?" asked the landlord quietly.

The tinker's eyes opened and his mouth opened, wider than one would have ever thought a man's eyes and mouth could open. Then his mouth stretched and his eyes almost closed. He dropped back on his stool and went into such roars of laughter as neither the landlord nor his good wife had ever heard before since they hired the inn. It was so loud and so long that the landlord began to beat the man on the back, and the landlady ran for water to throw into his face. Twice the tinker stopped, and twice he began again. The landlord actually gave a wary look at the timbers of the room to see whether they showed any signs of loosening from their places.

At last the tinker was sober enough to ask with not more than two chuckles to every word : —

Robin Hood: His Book

"Will you tell me where I can find him again?"

"You'll find him somewhere in the forest," answered the landlord.

"Here's the ten shillings," said the tinker, counting them out carefully from his leathern purse, "and will you keep my hammer and my working bag safe for me till I come again?"

"Willingly," promised the landlord, and the tinker went down the path. The landlord and his wife stood at the window. As the tinker closed the gate, they saw him bend almost double with a great guffaw of laughter that shook him like a bulrush; and from every little turn in the road that led to the forest, chuckles and cackles and giggles and titters came back to them on the wind.

Robin was not far away; indeed, he had said to himself : —

"If the jolly tinker is the man I think he is, he will come out to find me, and we'll have a good, friendly fight and see who's the better man of us two."

As the tinker drew near, Robin called out : —

"What knave is he that's coming so boldly into the forest?"

" Knave yourself," cried the tinker; but even then there was a queer little quaver in his voice that might easily have turned into a chuckle.

" Come out here and fight," called Robin. " What's your weapon ? "

" A good crab-tree staff," answered the tinker, "and it's a full match for that silly little sword of yours.   A sword is no weapon for a man, but if he has a good stout staff, he knows when he has hit something."

" And if he has a sword, the thing that is hit knows it," retorted Robin.

Then they fought.   The tinker laid on fast, and Robin laid on fast.   There was bout on bout, and then there was another bout.

" A truce," cried Robin ; so the tinker stopped with his crab-tree staff held high in the air.   " I 've thought of something," said Robin.   " If we keep on in this way much longer, we might hurt each other.   Then I 've thought of another thing, and it is n't often that a man has two thoughts in one day.   You're too good a fellow to go about mending pots and pans.   Come to the greenwood and be one of my own men.   You 'll have a cloak of the Lincoln green and a yew-tree bow, and a belt

Robin Hood: His Book

of arrows well winged with the gray goose-quill.
You 'll feast on venison, and you 'll drink as good
a wine as any that 's in the cellar of the sheriff.
What do you say ? "

" In faith, and I 'll do it, and here 's my hand on
it," answered the tinker.

" Come, then," said Robin, " and we 'll have our
supper.   There 's naught that makes a man so
hungry as fighting, and I told the landlord we 'd
be back in good time, and we 'd want the finest
supper he could get."

" And how did you know there 'd be two of
us ? " queried the tinker in amazement.

" I 've seen men before," quoth Robin.

VIII

ROBIN HOOD AND THE STRANGER

HE shadows had grown long in the forest. The slender blades of grass were already weighed down with the dew. The little birds had sung their last good-night. From the tree-top came the hoot of the great owl, and from the swamp far away echoed the lonesome wailing of the loon. The stars were beginning to show faintly through the branches. Robin Hood and Little John and William Scarlet were walking quietly along the forest path.

" Hist, Master," whispered Little John. " What might that be far down the road ? "

" Could it be a ghost ? " asked William Scarlet, peering into the shadow.

" It 's black," mused Robin. " They say a ghost is white and a goblin is brown."

Robin Hood: His Book

" I 'll slip on ahead through the trees and have a look at it," whispered William Scarlet.

He slipped through the trees as softly as a breath of air could have done, and soon he was back again.

" What is it?" asked Robin and Little John.

" It's no ghost and it's no goblin," said he, " but unless there's magic about it" — and here he rubbed his eyes and peered down the road — " unless there's magic about it, it's a maiden all alone on a black palfrey. The saddle is black and the bridle is black. She wears a black gown and over her face and falling down over her shoulders is a long black veil of Cyprus lawn. You can't always tell when a woman's grieving, but I'm almost sure I saw a tear roll down to the ground under her veil, and I heard her say ' Alas,' and then, before you could have shot an arrow, she said ' Alas ' again. It was a dolesome sight, Master, indeed it was."

" If she has lost her way," said Robin thoughtfully, " we can take her home safely; and if any one has stolen her from her friends and left her, we can shoot him ; and if any one has robbed her of gold and gone over seas, we can get more from the first abbot or bishop that comes this way. We must find out what it is, but she'd be frighted if we three came upon her all at once. One of us must go alone."

"Master Robin is the handsomest," said William Scarlet.

"Little John is the biggest," said Robin.

"But William Scarlet can make the finest bow," declared Little John; and so it was decided that William Scarlet should go to the weeping maiden on the palfrey, and ask her why it was that the tears were rolling down upon the ground from under her veil of Cyprus lawn.

Robin and Little John sat down on a log beside the road while William Scarlet followed on in the way that she had taken. The moon had come out, and they could see William bowing as he went along, now to one side and now to the other, for he meant to be sure that he would make his very best obeisance to the maiden on the palfrey.

It was a great pity that all the practising went for nothing, but truth to tell, when he came up beside her, he forgot all about his fine bow, for she had thrown off her black veil, and by the light of the rising moon William saw the reddest cheeks and the reddest lips and the bluest eyes and the whitest forehead that ever he had seen in all his life.

A man might well have counted a score while he stood looking at her, too dazed to speak. Then he saw that her eyes were so bright because there was a shining tear in each of them, and he said: —

" Fair lady, might there be aught that a simple bowman could do for you? Is it perhaps that you have lost your way in the forest?"

" No," answered the maiden, with a sigh. " I would it were."

" If it might be that any one has robbed you of gold, I have friends not far away, and we can catch the thief and hang him to the highest tree in the greenwood."

The maiden only shook her head.

" I would gladly give all the gold and lands that my father left me," said she, " if only I might be freed from my trouble."

She smiled so sadly, and her voice was so sweet, that William was puzzled, for he said to himself : —

" No man could ever leave a maiden like that ;" and then he made the fine bow that he had been practising all the way up the road, and asked a little anxiously: —

" Is it for some one that 's dear to you that you are grieving so sorely ? "

" Truly, yes," answered the maiden, " dearer than was ever a mistress to a maiden before."

" Oho," thought William, and he plucked up courage and asked boldly: —

" And what can I do for the mistress who is dear to you? Is she a great lady ? Is she the wife of a duke or an earl ? "

" She 's the daughter of the king," sobbed the maiden; and while William stood beside her and laid his hand on the neck of her palfrey and looked up into her face, she told him the whole story.

" It 's a heathen prince that has come against London town with his great army," said she. " They say he 's as tall as a poplar tree and as strong as an oak. There are two fearsome giants with him, and they are worse than he, for they are tall as the mast of a ship and as strong as iron. No one has dared to look at them, but the folk say that their eyes are like coals of fire, and that when they breathe, the leaves shrivel up and fall from the trees all roundabout. They say that on their helmets there are no plumes, but that instead there are great serpents, and that if

the giants cannot reach a man with their swords, then the serpents will spring away from the helmets and sting him, and whoever is once stung by them goes mad forever after."

"These be two good friends of mine," said

William Scarlet, for Robin and Little John had come up and stood beside him. "Whatever simple bowmen can do for you, that will we do."

"I thank you," said the maiden, "but I fear me there's none that can save my princess, for the heathen be encamped all about the town."

"Why does not the king take his army and go out and fight them?"

"That would he do if it was our own Richard," she answered, "but he that's now king says that he cannot, for he never fought so many men before."

The three looked puzzled, and at last Little John plucked up courage and said:—

"I'm but a simple country laddie, and it may be I don't understand the ways of city folk, but what might it be that's to happen to the princess?"

"The heathen prince says she's to be his bride, and that if the king does not send her to him before the moon rises on midsummer night, he and his two giants and his great army will tear down the city walls and burn every house and kill every man and woman and child in all London town."

"Is there no way of escape?" queried Robin.

Robin Hood: His Book

" Only this," answered the maiden sadly. " He says he has n't had a good fight for a whole year, and that if the king can bring out three strong men to fight him and his two giants, then if he loses he will ask no more for the hand of the princess."

" Master, let us — " began William Scarlet, but Robin asked : —

" And does the king not scour the country around for champions, and does he not offer a great weight of gold and the diamonds and pearls from his crown and the rubies and emeralds from his sceptre to any one that will save the princess ? "

" He says that no king was ever in such a strait before, and that he knows not what to do."

" And you are searching for three champions ? " asked William Scarlet.

The maiden bowed her head. " The heathen prince said that four of us who were the princess's bower maidens might go as we would, one north, one south, one east, and one west, and search well for champions; and they say he laughed a fearful laugh, and the serpents hissed, and the two giants beat their falchions."

"Has the princess no true lover who will be one of the three?" asked Robin.

"Surely she has," replied the maiden, "as brave a man as ever bore a sword, but he 's lying sick of a fever." The three men stood silently, and the maiden went on:—

"I must away, for the princess will fear that harm has come to me; and she has sorrow enough without grieving for the loss of one that is dear to her." The palfrey gave a bound, and before another word could be said, the maiden was out of sight.

Still the three men stood silent, and Robin looked so downhearted that Little John asked:—

"Master, might it be that the maiden's bright eyes have pierced your heart? If so it be, I'll go after her, and she shall be your bride; will she or will she not?"

"There's but one maiden in all the world for me," answered Robin; "and she's not the damsel on the black palfrey." Then Robin thought and thought. At last he said:—

"Shall we three men go forth as champions for the princess?"

"I'll be your second," cried William Scarlet.

"And I'll be your third," cried Little John.

"Never had a master such good followers," declared Robin; and he threw his arms around the neck of first one and then the other.

"It's but a little time that we have to make our way to London town," said William Scarlet. "Midsummer Day is but two risings of the sun away."

"We'll put off our green cloaks," said Robin, "and we'll don cloaks of gray. No swords and no shields will we take, but we'll carry long staffs in our hands, and by the side of each shall hang a scrip and a water bottle. Men will think we be three pilgrims just come from the Holy Land, or else three hermits come from our caves to go into the great church in London town, and no man will dare to stop us."

Then did they as Robin bade, and they walked boldly along the highway. As they went over the bridge and up the little hill, whom should they see but the sheriff of Nottingham! The proud sheriff turned meekly to the other side of the road, and bowed himself before them and said : —

"Greeting, Holy Fathers, and my humble reverence to you."

Robin Hood: His Book

"Greeting," quoth Robin, "and our blessing. The day is happier to us that we have passed you."

Down the long road they went as fast as ever they could, for the time was short. Hasten as they might, the lists were made ready before they were in sight of the town, and even before they were through the gates the trumpet had sounded, and the heathen prince had gone forth to demand his bride.

There were no serpents on his helmet, of course, and his eyes were not at all fiery, neither was his breath like the breath of a furnace; but any one could see that he was a great fighter. On either side of him was a tall man, and they were the two giants. Up and down the lists the three strutted.

"This is the morning of Midsummer Day," the prince shouted. "You have no champions. Bring forth my bride."

The queen wept, and the king groaned. Between them stood the princess, and she was white as marble. Not a tear did she shed, not even when she thought of him who lay sick of a fever; but deep in the pocket of her gown was a keen little dagger, for whatever others might say or do, she meant never to be the bride of the heathen prince.

"Have pity," moaned the queen, and "Have pity," moaned the king; but all the answer that the heathen prince made was to call louder than before, "Bring forth my bride, or London town burns to-morrow."

"Such a thing never happened to me before," wailed the king. "I don't know what I can do."

"For the third time I tell you to bring forth my bride," called the heathen prince.

The king took one step forward, leading the princess by the hand. He took another step, but before he could take the third, there was a little commotion at the farther end of the lists, and the herald cried: —

"There be three doughty champions come to fight for the princess!"

The people of London town shouted with delight and cheered until the lists rang; but when the three pilgrims appeared, each in a gray cloak, bearing a long staff in one hand, and with scrip and water bottle hanging at his side, then some of the Londoners laughed in scorn, and some wept with disappointment.

The three champions advanced and knelt before the king. Then said Robin : —

"We be three simple bowmen. We must be beholden to you for swords and shields, but we will gladly give our own blood and our lives to free the princess."

The king had presented arms to more than one good fighter before this, so now he knew just what to do. He sent for swords and lances and shields, great numbers of each. Robin and his men chose carefully, and then went forward to meet the heathen prince. The trumpets sounded, and the charge was made.

The swords flashed, and the shields rang with the heavy blows. Indeed, there was such flashing and shining and twinkling and sparkling and gleaming and glittering, and such ringing and clinking and clanging and banging and crashing and clashing, that when it all stopped, nobody knew at first exactly what had happened. In a moment they saw that one " giant " was nailed to the ground with a lance through his heart. A terrible sword-stroke had cleft the head of the other ; while, as for the prince himself, his body lay in the middle of the lists, but his head had rolled away into a dusty corner.

Then was there such shouting as had never been heard before, even on the tournament grounds of London town. The men cheered and waved their mantles, and the women waved their long silken sleeves and bunches of flowers and anything else that they could pick up.

The king had presided at many tournaments, so now he knew just what to do, and he came forward with a very fine little speech that he had often made before. He said that it was an excellent thing to have tournaments, and he told how many weighty questions had been decided by single combat. It occurred to him that he ought to thank the three champions for saving his daughter from marriage with the prince; but while he was trying to think what to say, the great army of the heathen learned that their leader was slain, and they ran away with all their might, so that the ground shook with the tramping, and not another word of the speech could be heard for their shouting.

Robin Hood: His Book

When all was quiet again, the king declared, "There must be a prize. There is always a prize at a tournament. It cannot be the hand of the princess, for she is already betrothed. What shall it be?"

"May I ask a boon for me and my men?" quoth Robin.

"Surely," answered the king, "and whatever you will, that shall you have."

"Then do I beg a free pardon for me and for my merrymen all," said he, "for I'm the outlaw Robin Hood."

"Pardon shall you have and welcome," promised the king, "and three new suits of clothes, and as much good yellow gold as you can carry away with you in three double handfuls."

So they were all rewarded, and London town was happy, and the princess was happy, and some one else was happy, too; for the first thing that the princess had done when she saw that the heathen prince lay dead was to send a swift messenger to the young man who was sick of a fever.

Robin made his obeisance to the king, and so did Little John, but William Scarlet hesitated.

Robin Hood: His Book

"Is there aught that you would ask of me? You shall have what you will." So said the king. Then spoke William Scarlet a little shyly : —

"Sir King, the brave maiden who went alone into the forest in search of champions for the princess — ought she not to be rewarded?"

"Indeed she ought," declared the king; and then the maiden who had ridden through the forest on the black palfrey was brought forward.

"The best reward that I can give to a brave maiden is a true husband," said the king thoughtfully; "and the best reward that I can give to a brave champion is a true wife. How is it, fair damsel, will you choose among these three champions for a husband?"

"I will do what your majesty bids me," answered the maiden meekly, but from under her eyelashes she looked shyly at William Scarlet.

"Shall we each ask in turn if she will have us?" quoth William Scarlet.

"Surely," answered the king; and he added with a sly twinkle in his eye, "It might be well for him that devised the scheme to be the first to speak."

Then said William Scarlet : —

"Fair maiden, might I hope that you will deign to look upon me?"

The maiden put out her lily-white hand to him, but suddenly the noble Earl of Maxfield arose and said: —

"The maiden has neither father nor brother, and I as her next of kin demand that he who would wed her shall prove that his birth is as good as her own. Her father was an earl, and her mother was a countess."

Then did every one gaze upon William Scarlet; but he, nowise daunted, stepped forward to the noble earl and said, "My father, too, is an earl, and my mother was a princess."

"Whose word will aver to that, young champion?"

"Will the word of one man be enough?" queried William Scarlet.

"So he be a man of honor," answered the earl.

"It is yourself that I call to bear witness," said William. "Was not your wife a princess, and had you not a son whom you called Gamwell? When his mother died, did he not in his wildness seek the forest? I am he."

"Many a day and night have I mourned his loss," said the earl, and then he looked William Scarlet full in the face, — "but how know I that you are he?"

Then William Scarlet looked full in the face of the Earl of Maxfield.

"In the northeast corner of your treasure-room," said he, "there is a secret door, and within that door, when the mortar was yet fresh in the wall, I laid my hand. Is there not in the wall the print of a child's hand?"

The earl bowed his head.

"There are two treasures hidden away behind that door. One is the portrait of my mother set with diamonds; the other is the portrait of myself set with rubies."

Then the earl knew that William Scarlet was really his son, for no one else had seen the treasures behind the secret door, and the next day the young man was married to the maiden. "For what can a man do but wed the maiden who has come out into the forest in search of him?" said the son of the Earl of Maxfield.

IX

ROBIN HOOD AND THE BUTCHER

"THANK you kindly, sir," said the little old woman to Robin Hood. " It 's more than once that you 've helped me, when the cow went dry and the pig died. It 's better than a pig that you 've been to me many and many a time, sir. And then there 's the good brown cloth that you gave me for a cloak, sir. There is n't another woman in town that has so fine a cloak. You 'd know it came from over the sea by the feel of it, and there 's folk in the town that has felt of it, too, and it was the sheriff's wife, it was. She came up, tossing her head with all the feathers on it, and followed me in through the door of the church to mass, and — "

" Did you go in through the door ahead of the sheriff's wife ? " interrupted Robin, with a merry twinkle in his eye.

"Truly, I did, sir. I said to myself, said I,
'Now I'm naught but a poor little old woman,
and I live in a hut with a thatched roof, and she
lives in a stone house; but when the great folk
give me such a fine cloak as this, it's but the
reverence that's due to them to take it into
the church before the rain might come to wet
it.'"

"And so you went ahead of the sheriff's wife!"

"I did that, and I felt the sheriff's wife a-
feeling of it when she went through the door.
You're good to me, indeed, sir. Will you come
into the cottage, and let me make you an oaten
cake?"

Robin went into the cottage, and sat down on
a wooden stool. The little old woman bustled
about, and stirred up the oaten meal and spread
it out thin on the board, and set it up before the
fire to bake. Then she pulled forward the iron
crane, and on the hook she hung a little iron pot
full of the nicest porridge that ever was made.
Very soon the porridge began to bubble, and the
oaten cake was brown as a berry.

"No, no, thank you humbly, sir," said she, "but
I'll not sit down, sir. I'll stand by your stool

and serve you. It's a proud woman that I am to have you sit at my table, and eat my oaten cake, and drink my porridge." So she poured more and more of the porridge into the wooden bowl, and put piece after piece of the oaten cake on the table beside it.

By and by Robin pushed the stool back from the table.

"So you walk into the church before the sheriff's wife," said he, "and you won't sit down at the table with a simple bowman like me that the sheriff thinks is only fit to be hanged."

"It's a humble little old woman that I am," she answered, "but it's the poor folk that know the real gentlefolk like you, sir. The sheriff's wife is naught but the wife of the sheriff."

"It's time for me to be going," said Robin. "Have you a bit of meat for your dinner?"

"It's oaten cake and porridge that I'll be having for my dinner," answered the little old woman simply.

"There's the butcher down the road," said Robin, shading his eyes, for the sun was coming up over the trees. "He's on his way to Nottingham, and we'll lighten his cart for

him; or should you rather have a bit of lightfoot?"

The little old woman began to tremble.

"Don't you, sir," she pleaded, "and don't you
be taking it amiss, but I'm afeard by week-days
and afeard by Sundays when I think of you.
Won't you get the king's pardon, sir, and then I'll
know you'll not be hanged on the gallows-tree?"

But Robin had gone down the road, and he
called to the butcher: —

"Hoot, man, have you a juicy slice of mutton that's fit to go under the finest cloak in
Nottingham?"

"Indeed, I have, and it's on its way to the wife
of the sheriff," called the butcher.

Robin looked closely at the man and asked
slyly: —

"Have you maybe a good bit of lightfoot hidden
away in that cart of yours?" Then the butcher
laughed and Robin laughed.

"It's all the fault of the little woman at home,"
said the butcher. "She said that she worrited by
day and worrited by night, and she sent me off to
get the king's pardon. The best of women have
a bit of foolishness in them."

Robin Hood : His Book

"And the better they are, the bigger it is," declared Robin gravely, "but it might be that a woman would give good advice. Here's the little old woman in the cottage yonder, she's been telling me to get the king's pardon; and when a woman wears a cloak like hers, a man must hearken well to what she says. I'll tell you what we'll do. I'll try being a butcher for a day. How much is your meat worth?"

"It might be one mark," answered the butcher.

"That's one, and the use of the horse is two, and the cart, three; and, oh, the frock and the cap. I'll borrow it all, and I'll give you four broad marks of gold. Do you take my good green cloak and my hunting-horn and my hat with the feather and bide with the little old woman till I come back. The sheriff sha'n't be hungering for his meat either. The best slice goes to the little old woman, but the next best goes to the wife of the sheriff, and I'll carry it to her myself."

"There's more than one that would grieve if you should fall into trouble," said the butcher.

"And why should one butcher fall into trouble more than another?" queried Robin lightly. "It might be that I'd bring the sheriff back with me. It's often enough that he's sought me to come to him."

Robin put on the long white butcher's frock and the little round cap, and into the cap he stuck a red rosebud, and then he set off for Nottingham.

"Good-by, good-by," he cried to the little old woman, but she only threw her apron over her face and crept into the house.

"Hold, here's the whip," called the butcher.

"Never a whip do I use for my beasts," cried Robin over his shoulder.

The good horse looked back at Robin. Then she switched her tail and winked her left ear at him, and they set off in the wildest gallop that ever carried a butcher's cart up the road to Nottingham. One wheel went over a log, and one went over a rock, and the pieces of meat bounded up into the air like hailstones that had struck a roof. The mutton hammered the beef, and the pork pounded the chicken, and again the good horse switched her tail and winked her left ear and galloped on to Nottingham. She dashed through the brook, she scrambled up the hill, she almost rolled down the hill, and the cart was now on one side of the road and now on the other. The ducks called " Quack, quack ! " The little dogs ran out to bark at the ducks, and scampered back with their tails between their legs. The cats sat on the fences ready to spit at the dogs, but the cats, too, ran for their lives without ever saying " Pst ! " The rooster strutted across the road, and the hens fluttered after him ; but they had no time to go back again, for the butcher's cart was upon them. The people in the cottages put their heads out of the windows ; but there was nothing to see except a great cloud of dust whirling up the road, so they crossed themselves and bolted the doors ; for perhaps the fiend himself was in that cloud of dust, they whispered to one another fearfully. And still the good horse switched her tail and winked her left ear and galloped on to Nottingham.

The keeper of the town gates flung them wide open, and in came Robin in his long white frock and white cap with the red rosebud in it. Every piece of meat lay still in its place, and the good horse arched her neck and went proudly up the street with the great white cart till she stood in the square in front of the sheriff's house.

Robin Hood: His Book

" Meat to sell, good meat to sell," cried Robin. The wife of the sheriff opened the door and came out on the steps.

" How much is your nice, juicy mutton ? " asked she.

" A penny a pound," quoth Robin.

" Give me four pounds," said the sheriff's wife quickly, for good mutton was full threepence a pound.

"Here's a pound weight," cried Robin, and in one hand he caught up a stone as big as his head while in the other he held the nice, juicy piece of mutton. " Here's a forequarter, that's one pound; and here's another forequarter, that's two pounds. Here's a hindquarter, that's three; and here's the other hindquarter, that's four."

Then the sheriff's wife ran into the house as fast as she could run to get the sheriff to carry in the meat, for she had no mind to lose such a bargain as that. The sheriff came out and made sure of the two forequarters and the two hindquarters, all for fourpence.

Robin went on calling, " Meat to sell, good meat to sell ; " and again the sheriff's wife came out on the steps and asked : —

How much is your nice juicy mutton? asked the Sheriff's Wife.

"How much is your good, tender beef?" and Robin answered:—

"A penny a pound, but I'm to have my own dinner of it."

The sheriff sat behind the shutters, and he whispered to his wife:—

"Ask him to dinner. I've thought of something."

"Will you come to dinner with us?" asked the sheriff's wife. "I'll buy your beef for a penny, and give you a dinner from it."

"Ay, that will I gladly," answered Robin heartily.

"Come when the sun is on the noon mark in the square," said she; and the sheriff whispered to her from behind the shutter:—

"I know him, I know him. It takes a wise man to be a sheriff, and I can tell who he is."

The other butchers had been gazing with their mouths and their eyes wide open, and one whispered to another:—

"The man's on a wager; he's no butcher."

"Yes, he is," said the other softly, "but the poor fellow's mad."

"Let's get him away," said the first, "before the sheriff cheats him out of every penny."

"We'll ask him to dine with us," suggested a third. "We'll find where he lives, and when the sheriff is taking his nap, we'll carry him home." So one of them went up to Robin and said:—

"We be all butchers together, sir, and we've come to ask you to eat dinner with us at the little inn beside the oak-tree."

"Thank you kindly," responded Robin. "He's no true man who'll deny one of his own trade. Shall we dine one hour before the sun is on the noon mark in the square?"

"Yes," answered they; and an hour before the sun was on the noon mark in the square, they all went away to the inn. They called for ale and beer and black pudding; but soon Robin began to call, and he called for fish and fowl and veal and marrow pasties and beef and cheese-cakes and tansy-cake and syllabub and jelly and junket and meat and sack. Never in all their lives had the butchers eaten such a dinner.

"However shall we pay the reckoning?" they began to whisper, but Robin kept on calling; and now there came in so many bottles of the innkeeper's best wine that the good butchers soon forgot all about the reckoning, and they did not even notice when Robin slipped out of the door and left them all sitting around the table.

"Here's a five-pound note for the dinner," he said to the innkeeper, and the innkeeper said:—

"Will you kindly come again, sir?"

"That will I," replied Robin. "Never a day will I sell meat in Nottingham that I do not have a dinner at your own good inn."

It was almost noon by the mark in the square when Robin walked boldly up to the sheriff's front door.

"Come in, come in," called the sheriff. "There's always a welcome for good true men like you."

"I'm grateful for your courtesy," said Robin. "When a man's but a simple butcher, he's humbly thankful for a great man's kindness."

"Oho," roared the sheriff. "It's a witty fellow that you are. There's no man that likes a good jest better than myself."

"Truly, Master Sheriff," said Robin gravely, "if I'm not a butcher, what am I then? Must not a poor man have some trade?"

"Oh, *I* know well who you are," cried the sheriff, "and there 's no man in Nottingham that would be more welcome to my house."

Then in came the sheriff's wife. She wore a blue silk gown that dragged behind her an ell or more. She had beads about her neck and rings on her fingers and a feather in her hair; and it was all to do honor to Robin, for the sheriff had said to her: —

"Put on your best blue silk gown, and put beads around your neck and rings on your fingers and a feather in your hair. I know who he is. His father owned the wide lands to the west of us, and he had the best herd of horned beasts in all Yorkshire. Bring out the oldest wine from the north side of the cellar. The son 's naught but a prodigal, and it won't be my fault if those wide lands and that herd of horned beasts are n't my own before I 'm a day older. We 'll give him wine till his head turns, and then I 'll say, ' Have you any horned beasts to sell?' and I 'll say, ' Have you any good land to sell?' and I 'll get his fine herd of cattle, and I 'll get his land, I will, and it 'll cost me little save the wine that he 'll drink."

"It 's a pity to waste the best wine," said the sheriff's wife, "and I think, if I 'd only held on a bit, I might have had the mutton for twopence instead of four."

" We 'll try to make it up on the land," said the sheriff.

All three sat down to the table. There was the roast beef, and there was not very much besides, for the sheriff's wife had thought: —

" What is the use of wasting a good dinner on a man who 'll drink so much wine that he 'll not know whether he 's had anything to eat or not ? "

Robin had some black bread and a piece of roast beef. It was not the best piece either, for the sheriff thought: —

" He 'll be but a beggar in an hour from now, and it won't take so much good wine to turn his head if he 's had little to eat."

Very soon the wine was brought in. Each of them had a wooden cup with a silver rim, and the sheriff filled the cups again and again.

" He 's drunk twice as much as I," said the sheriff to himself in great delight, for he did not know that Robin had poured two glasses out of every three down upon the rushes under the table. Pretty soon the sheriff's wife touched her husband's foot, and he began :—

"And so you 're playing at being a butcher?"

"Yes," said Robin, rather sleepily.

"You sell good meat, but have you by chance any horned beasts to sell?" The sheriff's wife gave a nod and a smile that meant :—

"How well he is doing it!" and Robin answered gravely :—

"Yes, Master Sheriff, I have horned beasts; it might be two or three hundred of them."

"I 'm not buying cattle, but young men like you often need a bit of money, and if you are anxious to sell, I might take them, just to help you along."

The sheriff's wife nodded a deeper nod and smiled a wider smile than before, and the sheriff went on boldly :—

"Perhaps you have a little land that you want to get rid of? Of course you could buy it back again some day, but I 'll take it of you now, if you will. It is n't every man that would do it, but I 'm always ready to oblige a friend in need."

The sheriff's wife nodded till one of her feathers fell off, and when she left the table to fasten it on again, she smiled so loud that Robin asked :—

" What was that ? "

" Oh, only the cackling of the hens under the window," answered the sheriff.   " And now," said he, " you want the money right away; young folk are always in a hurry; and if you 'll take me in your butcher's cart, we 'll go and see the horned beasts and the bit of land."

Then the sheriff and Robin climbed up into the cart.   Again the good horse switched her tail and winked her left ear, and again she galloped away over logs and rocks and brooks, up hill and down hill.

" But this is the road to the forest," cried the sheriff in alarm.

" It 's the nearest way to my herd of horned beasts," said Robin.

The sheriff was badly frightened, for he thought: " Surely, the fellow 's mad," but he could call upon no one for help, for the gates were fastened, and the doors were bolted, and the shutters of every house that they passed were closed tight.   Every man that lived on the road had crossed himself and crept into bed when he heard the wild galloping, for he had thought, " One may escape the fiend once, but not twice."

The sheriff trembled, and clung to the seat to keep from falling out of the cart. Then they turned into the forest road, and now the sheriff trembled so that he shook the cart.

"The saints preserve us from Robin Hood," cried he. "Are you sure that your horned beasts are here?" Just then a herd of deer flashed by.

"Those are my horned beasts," said the wild young butcher, "and all around us is the good free land, and if you 'll have it, I 'll give you as good a title to it as my father gave to me."

"He 's surely mad," moaned the sheriff; and as they came to a little cottage, he called out: —

"Help, help! Save me from the madman!"

It was the little old woman's cottage. She came running to the door, and when she saw the sheriff, she, too, set up a screaming and a screeching: —

"Oh, Master Robin, Master Robin! The sheriff 's got him, the sheriff 's got him, and he 'll be hanged on the gallows-tree. Oh, oh, oh!"

The real butcher man sat in a corner of the little old woman's cottage, and now he put his head out of the window and blew a long, long blast on Robin's horn. There was a sound of tramping through the woods, and in a minute, Little John and his merry company were with them.

"What is your will, Master?" asked they.

"I think it is the sheriff that wants to see you," said Robin soberly.

The sheriff was whiter than the butcher's frock. He had fallen down on his knees, and was shaking more than he had shaken when the cart jolted over the logs and over the rocks. Not a word said Robin's men, but every one of them slowly fitted an arrow to his bow and aimed it at the sheriff.

"Master, shall we shoot?" asked they.

"I'm afraid you might hit him," answered Robin. "We'll just send him home with a present for his wife. It's she that likes good mutton, and we'll send her a fourpenny bit." Then a forequarter of mutton was tied upon the sheriff's right shoulder and another forequarter upon his left shoulder.

"Take a hindquarter in each hand," bade Robin, " and go you straight home to your wife."

So the sheriff went stumbling and staggering under the weight up the long road to the gates of

Robin Hood: His Book

Nottingham. He did not dare to drop his burden, for Robin had said : —

"It's not fitting for a great man like the sheriff to journey over the land alone, and we 'll give him a goodly band of followers, four and twenty of the best bowmen in the country ; " and whenever the sheriff stopped a minute to rest, an arrow would whiz by his ear, and Robin would call out : —

"It's not courtesy to keep a great lady waiting for a little fourpenny gift like that."

X

ROBIN'S FAST DAY

'M thinking that we 'll have no dinner to-day."

" Why, Master, there 's as rare a haunch of venison as ever ran the forest, and there 's a marrow pasty, and there 's warden pie, and there 's some of the best wine that ever lay in the cellar of the sheriff of Nottingham."

" Still, I 'm thinking that we 'd best eat no dinner. I 've not yet been paid the four hundred pounds that I gave to the knight."

" And sha'n't we ever have any dinner till he pays it ? " asked William Scarlet dismally.

" I don't want him to pay it," declared Robin, " and if he brings it, we 'll pack it in a roll of silk and send it for a present to his wife."

Little John beckoned to Friar Tuck and whispered : —

[141]

"Was he ever this way before?" Friar Tuck shook his head.

"It was to save his son from the gallows-tree," said Robin, "and the stout Abbot of Saint Mary's lent him four hundred pounds on his land, and we gave him the money to pay the stout Abbot."

"Truly, yes, Master," said Friar Tuck.

"Then it's our four hundred pounds that has gone to the stout Abbot, and it's not willing that I am to believe the Blessed Virgin will let a man like him keep the good gold unless we've done somewhat that might offend her; so we'll just fast a day, and mayhap she'll forgive us and send us the four hundred pounds."

The men looked silently at Robin. Then said Friar Tuck:—

"You would n't be expecting a messenger to come all this way into the forest, would you, Master?"

"It might be not," answered Robin thoughtfully. Then said Friar Tuck:—

"I'm thinking I'll go out to Watling Street, Master."

"And I'll go with you," declared William Scarlet.

"And I, too," cried Little John.

Then Friar Tuck and William Scarlet and Little John set out for Watling Street.

"You've something in your mind, Friar Tuck."

"I've more in my mind than in my stomach," said Friar Tuck mournfully.

"And what might it be that's in your mind, Friar Tuck?" asked Little John. "Might it be what will mayhap put something into your stomach?"

"There's more than one person, and there's more than one thing to be found on the highway," said Friar Tuck, "and it might be that the messenger of the Blessed Virgin's among them;" and not another word would he speak until they were close upon Watling Street. Then said he:—

"We'll just slip down behind the hedge, and if the Blessed Virgin sends a messenger, we'll be ready to meet him." So there they lay, looking through a gap, to watch for the messenger with the four hundred pounds of gold.

The first that came along was a parish priest, but suddenly the good priest dropped down on his knees and began to say a prayer that the evil spirits might be kept away from him.

"No one but a fiend would shoot arrows at a poor priest," said he, for an arrow had whizzed through the air above his head and had made a little cloud of dust in the road.

"I'll carry it to the church and sprinkle it with holy water," he thought; and he picked up the arrow. Then he was the happiest priest in all Watling Street, for tied to the arrow was a broad goldpiece.

"It's no one but Robin that would do that," said he to himself joyfully, "and now the Widow Gill shall have a new roof for her cottage."

All this time the three men were hiding behind the hedge, watching for the one that should bring the four hundred pounds of gold.

"Think you that yon old woman's the messenger?" quoth Little John; for down the highway was an old woman, all bent and bowed, struggling to carry a bundle of dead sticks from the forest.

"Greeting," called Friar Tuck, stepping out into the road.

"Greeting, sir," said the old woman; and then she laid her great bundle down by the side of the way, so she could make a curtsey to the fine gentleman.

"That's a heavy bundle," said Friar Tuck.
"Where do you live?"

"In the cottage that's at the bottom of the
third hill from here, sir."

"Should you be afraid if you heard three men
going round about your cottage the first dark
night?"

The old woman looked closely into the man's
face and whispered softly: —

"There's none of the poor folk, sir, that'll feel
fear of Master Robin and his men."

"Then the first dark night there'll be three
men going round about the cottage, and when
you open the door in the morning, you'll see a
pile of wood; and the next dark night there'll be
more, till you have enough for the winter."

"The saints bless you," whispered the old
woman, "and bless the kind-hearted man that
you serve."

Then again the three men hid behind the
hedge to watch for the one that should bring
the four hundred pounds of gold.

"Think you that yon man riding up the
little hill is the messenger?" asked William
Scarlet.

"It's the proud sheriff himself," answered Friar Tuck.

Not a finger did one of them move till the sheriff had come up the hill, and was but across the road. Then Little John let fly an arrow that whizzed over the man's right shoulder.

The sheriff turned pale, and he ran for his life; but however fast he ran on one side of the hedge, Little John and Friar Tuck ran just as fast on the other. One arrow flew over his left shoulder, and another over his head. They whizzed and buzzed, and hissed in his ears.

"Murder, murder," cried the sheriff. "There are a hundred of them, and they're all shooting at me." The sheriff ran and tumbled and rolled down the hill with all his might and main, and the three men dropped down behind the hedge and laughed to see him go.

"Methinks the messenger's long o' coming," said Little John dolefully, "and we'll have no dinner till he does come."

"It's a great thing to eat a dinner that costs four hundred pounds," said William Scarlet.

"I doubt me that any one but the king does

that," declared Little John meditatively, "and I don't feel sure that he does it every day."

"A bit of black pudding would n't be bad eating," suggested William Scarlet.

"And I could swallow some good wheaten flummery as well as if I were a great man," added Friar Tuck.

"The little old woman in the cottage over the third hill would cook us an oaten cake and gladly," said William Scarlet.

"And leave Master Robin to fast by himself?" cried Little John.

"Fasting is all very well, but a man should n't do it on an empty stomach," declared Little John gravely.

"I 'll climb the oak-tree and look north and south and east and west," said Friar Tuck, and halfway up the tree he went. Then he dropped softly to the ground and whispered: —

"He 's coming, he 's coming, and I 'll warrant he 's brought the four hundred pounds. Look down over the hill."

"It 's a monk," whispered William Scarlet, "and see the fine palfrey he 's on. Look at the seven sumpter mules, and see the two and fifty men-at-arms that ride after them. There is n't a noble in all the land that rides so like a king."

"Brothers," said Little John, "we be three hungry men, and in the packs of the mules or else in the bag of the monk lies our dinner."

"Three can't fight two and fifty," declared William Scarlet.

"No," agreed Friar Tuck thoughtfully, "but I 've heard tell that sometimes if a man shows courtesy, it 's as good as fighting. If he 's the messenger coming to bring us our dinner, it 's only right to go out and meet him."

So Friar Tuck smoothed his hair and shook out the folds of his hunting cloak, and when the monk, followed by the seven sumpter mules and the two and fifty men-at-arms, had come near, the Friar stepped out into the road, pulled off his hunting cap, and bowed him low before the noble company.

"Sir Monk," said he, with another bow deeper than the first, "might it be that you are a messenger to my master?"

"Do I look like a man with a message, you stupid wood-ranger?" demanded the monk indignantly.

Robin Hood : His Book

"Indeed, I'm not sure," answered Friar Tuck doubtfully, "but my master sends you courteous greeting, and bids you come and dine with him."

"Who is your master?" asked the monk a little more politely, for who could tell whether this might not after all be the servant of some lord of high degree?

"Robin Hood is my master's name," answered Friar Tuck.

"He's an outlaw and a thief," declared the monk, "and I never yet heard word or deed of him that was good."

Again Friar Tuck bowed low before him.

"The little path just beyond the gap in the hedge is the way into the forest," said the Friar. "Would it please you to look at it?" The monk looked, but his glance did not go beyond the hedge, for there he saw two shining arrows aimed full at himself.

"Help!" he began to call, but the Friar said meekly: "I know it's not the place of a humble serving-man to give advice to a great monk, but I'm fearful the arrows might fly before the men could come. One never knows where his arrow will go, and I 'm greatly afraid they might strike you."

Paler and paler turned the monk. Then quoth Friar Tuck, standing humbly with his cap in his hand : —

"Would it not be better, sir, to make sure of one good dinner? There 's as fine a haunch of venison as ever ran the forest, and there 's a marrow pasty, and there 's warden pie, and there 's good wine to wash it down. Will you not come with me to dinner, sir?"

The monk's teeth chattered with fear. He glanced at the two arrows, and he said very humbly : —

"I will go with you." Then said Friar Tuck regretfully : —

"My master would gladly show courtesy to your men-at-arms, but he 's had no new silver trenchers of late, and he cannot well entertain so great an array. Will you say to them that they are to go back to York and await your coming?"

The monk glanced again at the arrows shining over the hedge, and he trembled so that he almost fell from his fine palfrey.

" Say, ' I 'm bidden to dine with a good friend,' " whispered Friar Tuck, and the monk repeated the words as best he could.

" Say, ' You may go back to York and await my coming,' " whispered Friar Tuck, and the monk said it, though his lips turned fairly blue.

" Now say this to the pages with the sumpter mules," whispered Friar Tuck. " Say, ' The pages with the sumpter mules may follow me. I shall perchance wish to make a gift to my good host.'"

Then the two and fifty men-at-arms galloped away over the hills to the town of York, but more than one of them gave a look over his shoulder back to the edge of the forest, and more than one grinned broadly as he whispered a word to the man who rode next him. It was a very cheerful company that went through the gates of York that morning.

The monk that had been invited to dinner, and the seven sumpter mules that were driven by the little page, and the three good bowmen and true all set out to go down the forest road.

Soon they came to Robin and Much the miller's son, and the others of the merry company.

"Master," said Friar Tuck, "we 've brought you a great man for a guest."

"Welcome, Sir Monk," said Robin with all courtesy. "Might it be that you come from Nottingham?"

"From York," answered the monk.

"And what is your abbey?" queried Robin.

"Saint Mary's," said the monk.

"Then, truly, you be the very messenger that

we have awaited," declared Robin. "Have you perhaps the four hundred pounds of gold that the Blessed Lady will send me?"

Now, frightened as the monk was, he had no mind to lose his money if he could help it, and he answered : —

"I'm no messenger, and I've but twenty marks."

"It's not good breeding to ask questions between meals," said Robin, "so we'll just have our dinner. I'll call my good men and true."

Then Robin sounded his horn, and galloping through the forest came seven-score good yeomen, every one of them wearing a fine mantle of cloth of scarlet and gray, and every one with a good yew-tree bow and a quiver full of shining arrows. Each man made a reverence to Robin, and then they all sat down to the feast. On one side of the monk sat Robin, and on the other sat Little John.

"Have some of the venison," said Robin; but the monk's hands trembled so that Robin had to put the tender bits into his mouth for him.

"Have some of the good wine," said Little John; but the monk's hands trembled so that

Little John had to hold the cup up to his lips for him.

If only the monk had not been so frightened, he would have known that it was the best feast he had ever seen in all his life. As it was, he was as sorry to have it come to an end as were any of Robin's good men, for he knew not what would be done with him. At last Robin asked, " Have you had all that you can eat ? " and he answered " Yes." Little John asked, " Have you had all that you can drink ? " and he answered " Yes." Then he was more frightened than ever, for all the men sat around on the grass, looking at him and looking at Robin. Robin said : —

" If you 've but a scant twenty marks, you 're ill provided for your journey, and I 'll gladly lend more to Our Lady's true and faithful servant." Robin spoke so gently that the monk began to take courage, and to think, " What a fool I was to be afraid ! " so he said aloud : —

" Truly, it is but a small sum for even a simple monk to journey on to Nottingham and back again to York."

" Then I 'll willingly lend you more," offered Robin.

Robin Hood: His Book

Now the monk felt very brave, and he thought, "What a fine story it will be to tell the abbot if I can go back with one hundred pounds more than I brought," so he said: —

"Thank you kindly, Master Robin. If you would lend me five-score or mayhap six-score pounds, it would be a courtesy to Our Lady, and I doubt not that you 'd get a blessing for the good deed."

"That will I do and most heartily," said Robin, "but it is our custom here in the forest never to lend money till we see for ourselves that a man has none of his own. Little John, will you open the leathern bag that lies across the neck of the palfrey?"

Little John spread out his green cloak on the ground under an oak-tree. Then he opened the leathern bag of the monk and told out one gold-piece after another, till on one side of the cloak was a pile of four hundred pieces, and on the other was another pile of four hundred pieces.

"Master," cried Little John, "Our Lady has paid you well. Here be the four hundred pieces that you lent her, and here be other four hundred pieces."

Robin Hood: His Book

"It's but one pile that belongs to me," said Robin, "and now that I've had my pay, I'll not keep the pile on the other side of the cloak, and I'll not keep the seven sumpter mules. The monk shall have all his way to Nottingham paid and his way back to York paid, and he shall spend not one of the yellow goldpieces in the other pile, for my own good men shall go with him so he shall be at no charge for men-at-arms."

Then the monk was set on his own palfrey and was led out of the forest with his four hundred pounds of gold and his seven sumpter mules.

"Farewell," called Robin, "and may your abbot send us such a monk every day in the year."

The monk left the forest and rode down the highway toward Nottingham town. He had not his two and fifty men-at-arms, but on one side of him rode Little John, and on the other rode Much the miller's son. It was a long way to Nottingham, but the sumpter mules could make no complaint, for at every cottage that they passed Little John would say to the monk, "Now throw out a goldpiece, and a good bundle of cloth;" and there were so many cottages that before they came to Nottingham, half the goldpieces and half the burden of the sumpter mules had been given to the poor people along the way.

"The air of the town is not good for a man's health," declared Much the miller's son, "so we'd best not go into Nottingham, but we'll go all the way back to York with our good friend, lest harm come to him on the journey."

Back to York they went, and just as it was on the way to Nottingham, so it was on the way to York, for at every poor little cottage the monk had to drop a goldpiece and a good roll of cloth. He had never had so many blessings from poor people in all his life, but his face grew longer and longer, for he feared what Little John and Much the miller's son might yet do to him before he was safe in York.

He need not have been afraid, for as the little company drew near the city walls Little John bent low before him and said:—

"Our master's greeting to the stout abbot of Saint Mary's. Wish him joy that he serves the Blessed Lady who never forgets a debt to even a simple bowman of the greenwood."

XI

ROBIN AND SIR GUY OF GISBORNE

"ASTER ROBIN," said Little John, "I 'm a-thinking that I 'll go to Bernisdale."

"Go where you will," replied Robin, "but see that you come back to me safe and sound. I 've heard that the proud sheriff is not so far from Bernisdale, and little could I spare that head of yours."

"I 'd be hard put to do without it myself, Master," answered Little John, "and mayhap you could spare it better than I; for it might well be that you could get another to serve you, but I 'm not so sure that I 'd find one to serve me."

Little John set out for Bernisdale, but when he came to the edge of the forest he stopped and thought.

"The guest that is unbidden would better be sure of his welcome. It 's not always well to come upon a great man unawares. It might be that the proud sheriff would be at a feast, and he would n't be pleased to give over drinking his nut-brown ale and his ruby-red wine just to come out and hang one wee laddie. I 'll go to the top of the bit hillock and see whatever is going on in Bernisdale town."

So Little John climbed to the top of the hill and looked over the moor to Bernisdale.

"What might the people be about in the market-place?" he said to himself. "There 's the proud sheriff, and round about him are full seven-score men. I fear me that such a meeting bodes but little good to us of the greenwood, for now I bethink myself, it 's this very path that our own William Scarlet took when he went away from us in the early red of the morning. They 're putting up a gallows-tree. Oh, but the man 's free! Run, man, run for your life!" he cried, forgetting that no one could hear his call.

The man ran over the moor, through the bushes, across the swamp and across the meadow-land. He sprang over the creek, he leaped from rock to rock, he jumped from hummock to hummock, he swung from tree to tree; and after him came the proud sheriff and his seven-score men, all scurrying over the plain.

They ran and they scampered and they rushed. They rolled down hill and they tumbled up hill. They bumped against the trees, they floundered in the swamp, they tangled themselves in the briar, they toppled over the rocks, they stumbled over the molehills, and they sprawled into the creek. They tripped one another up. They slipped, and they lurched, and they slid, and they pitched, till six-score men and one were scattered over the country between the town of Bernisdale and the greenwood as if they were so many huckle-berries; and only the proud sheriff and a score of his followers save one were left to pursue the man that was running to the greenwood.

Little John stood at the end of the path where it came out from the forest in a narrow valley be-tween two high, rocky walls.

"Oh, William, William!" he shouted; for as the man came nearer he saw that it really was their own William Scarlet. "Run, William, run! Not this path, the one to the left; it's far shorter. Run, run! I 'll hold them back, run!" William ran as never man ran before, and when the sheriff and his score of followers save one came up, puffing and blowing and gasping for breath, he was nowhere in sight, and the only person to be seen in the forest was a tall country lad lying asleep under a tree.

"Where's the man?" they cried, "the man that ran by here but now?"

"Was there any man?" asked Little John, getting up clumsily and rubbing his eyes. "No man went down this path, Masters. I'm going home to get my dinner;" and he stumblingly made his way to the path that came out between the two high, rocky walls.

"You'll be a dinner yourself for the ravens and the kites," roared the sheriff, "if you don't tell me the truth. Did he go down this path?"

"I saw a man on this path one day," answered the country lad, still rubbing his eyes.

"Was it this morning?"

"If you'll let me think a bit, mayhap I could remember," said Little John, as he stretched himself up and yawned, — and all this time William Scarlet was running for his life down the other path, — "yes, it was this morning; but it might have been somebody else."

"You 're somebody else yourself," said the sheriff suddenly. "I know you now. You 're no stupid country lad; you 're another of Robin Hood's men. Another is as good as one, and we 'll just hang you instead of him."

"Will you, though?" cried Little John. "Then I 'll have a shot or two at you first;" and in a moment his bow was bent, and an arrow was set, already to pierce the proud sheriff to the heart; but just as the arrow left the string, the good bow that had never failed before snapped in twain. There stood Little John, and in front of him was the sheriff with his score of men save one.

Far off over the moor Little John could see the town of Bernisdale, and there stood the gallows-tree that had been built to hang William Scarlet.

"I 'll not be hanged without good reason," cried Little John. One man he dashed against the rock on his right, another against the rock on his left; and one he threw over either shoulder. Two men he caught in each hand and knocked their four heads together till no one of the four knew which was his own. Two men he laid on the ground like stepping-stones in a brook, and then he stood on their backs and went on fighting. One man he struck with a stone and another with the branch of a tree. The sheriff and seven men were left, and every one of them stood with an arrow well aimed at Little John.

" Now will you yield, and come and be hanged on the gallows-tree ? " cried the sheriff.

" It 's many a time that you 've sought me to come and be your guest at the gallows-tree. Mayhap it 's but scant courtesy always to answer you nay, so I 'll go with you, lest you should never have so good a chance to ask me again."

The sheriff and his men were so afraid that Little John would get away that they tore up their cloaks and their tunics to make bonds to tie his hands behind his back.

" In faith, I 'm ashamed to go into the town with such a ragged company," quoth Little John. " When we invite you to the greenwood, Master Sheriff, we put on our best clothes to do you honor, but it 's little honor you show to your own invited guest."

" Oh, we 'll honor you, never fear for that," laughed the sheriff loudly, for he was in the best of spirits. "We'll give you the highest place of all, and if any one tries to take you away, we'll stand by you to a man."

Across the moor they went, and as they marched on, one after another joined them of the six-score men and one that lay scattered over the plain like huckleberries. They were bruised by the rocks and bumped by the trees and scratched by the briars and lamed by the pitfalls and mired by the swamps; and it was a shabby looking company that limped and shambled and lumbered and tottered and staggered and crept and hobbled and crawled and finally made their way into Bernisdale town.

"Now mount the gallows, and see you delay not," bade the sheriff. " It is n't every guest that has the highest place at the feast. If I let you slip through my fingers this time, may you never come this way again."

"That's a right good wish," said Little John, "and, truly, I thank you for it, for it might be that it would come to pass." He looked eagerly along the edge of the forest, but there was no sign of Robin Hood. Just then a horn blew faintly far in the greenwood.

Robin Hood: His Book

"I would that were my master's horn," whispered Little John to himself, "but it's all up with me now."

The rope was put about his neck, and the sheriff called : —

"One, two —" Then the horn blew again.

"Stop," shouted the sheriff. "That's the horn of Sir Guy of Gisborne. He set out in the dew of the morning, and he swore to me fast and true that when I heard the blast of his horn, I should know that he was bringing a prisoner to town, and the name of the prisoner should be Robin Hood."

"Then let us wait, Master Sheriff," suggested one of his men, "and build another gallows and hang them both together, this man on one and Robin Hood on the other."

"That's a merry thought," said the sheriff. "Take the fellow down. Tie him fast to the post of the gallows-tree, and when we come back we'll have such a rejoicing as there never was before in all the country round."

So Little John was tied fast to the gallows-tree, and the sheriff and all of his men that could creep or crawl went out to meet Sir Guy of

Gisborne and help him bring Robin Hood into Bernisdale town to be hanged.

That selfsame morning Robin was wandering up and down in the forest, when under an oak-tree he saw standing alone a man in brown.

"Good morrow," said Robin. "It's a fine bow you have, and by the look of it you should be a good archer. Shall we set up a mark and try our skill together?"

" No shooting for me," answered he in brown, " till I come to the man that I want to shoot at; but I'm doubtful of my way, and it might be that you could tell me on which side of the forest lies the town of Bernisdale. If you can, I'll give you a silver penny."

"The man that bides in the greenwood has little need for silver pennies," said Robin cheerily, " but I've had no trial with the bow for three long days, and if you will, we'll set up a willow wand and see who is the better marksman. Then, if it please you, I'll show you willingly and without any silver penny the nearest way to Bernisdale."

The willow wand was set up three-score rods away.

" Lead on, my good fellow," said Robin. " The first shot is your own."

" Nay, but lead yourself," bade the man in brown. So Robin stepped out and bent his bow, and his arrow struck close by the side of the wand. Then shot the man in brown, and his arrow was a full three-fingers' breadth away, while Robin's next shot split the wand, and the two pieces flew apart, and fell one on either side of the tree.

" If you shoot like that all the time," said the man in brown, " you 're a better bowman than Robin Hood himself."

" And what know you of him ? " asked Robin.

" Only that it 's for him that I 've come out this morning a sworn man, for I 've vowed to take the outlaw bold if once I set eyes on him. If you dwell in the forest, it might be that you could tell where he bides."

" It might be," quoth Robin gravely.

" If you 'll but show me one little glimpse of him within the length of a bowshot, I 'll give you forty silver pounds."

" I 've no more use for your forty silver pounds than I had for your one silver penny," answered

Robin, " but I 'd gladly be good friends with the man I 've shot with. If you 'll come to the wee bit shelter that I 've put up here in the forest, I 'll willingly share a morsel of bread and a cup of ale with you. It 'll hinder you but a moment, and then I 'll go part way with you to Bernisdale."

"No time have I for bread and ale," returned he in brown ungraciously. " It 's not bread and ale that I 'm after, it 's the bold outlaw and the hundred pounds of silver that the sheriff will bring when he hears the sound of my bugle-horn and knows that I 've taken Robin Hood."

" But why do you seek to take the life of Robin Hood? Has he done aught of harm to you or yours? "

" No harm has he done to me or mine," answered the man in brown.

" Is he not loyal to the king? Does he not go to the mass whenever the proud sheriff is from home? Is there ever a maiden that he has stolen away or a parish priest that he has hurt? Has he ever burned a haystack or robbed a husbandman of beast or crop? Has he ever slain a man save in a fair fight? "

Robin Hood: His Book

" He's an outlaw and a robber," retorted the man in brown.

" Has he ever taken from the rich that he did not give to the poor ? "

" What business is it of yours ? " suddenly demanded he in brown. "One would think you were one of the outlaw's own men."

" But I'm not," answered Robin quietly.

" Tell me your name," shouted the other fiercely.

" Nay, but tell me your own first," said Robin.

" No need have I to hide my name. It's Guy of Gisborne, and I'm known throughout the countryside. Many an outlaw have I brought to the sheriff and the gallows-tree ; and when I sound on my bugle-horn, the sheriff and seven-score men will come out from Bernisdale, and it's a hundred good silver pounds that they will bring, and they'll hang the thief on the gallows-tree. I'm thinking that it's built high and strong by this time o' the day."

" And would you hang a man that's done no harm to you or yours ? Would you hang him just to get the silver pounds ? "

Robin Hood: His Book

"Ay, that I would," declared Guy of Gisborne.

"Would you give him no chance for a fair fight?"

"Fair!" cried Guy of Gisborne. "Naught is it to me whether it's fair or not. I'd shoot him down like a wolf. It's not a fight that I want, it's the mickle silver."

"Once more I ask you, Sir Guy of Gisborne, if I show you safely to the forest's edge, will you either go back to Bernisdale, or else will you promise to give Robin a fair fight if you meet him in the greenwood?"

"I tell you it's the mickle silver that I want," said Sir Guy impatiently. "I care naught whether a fight's fair or unfair."

"Once then in your life, and it may be only once, shall you fight fairly," exclaimed Robin, fitting an arrow to the string. "I am Robin Hood. I will fight for my life, and you may fight for the silver. A life like your own is not worth fighting for. Lay down your bow. Go you to the thicket on the left and cut as stout a club as you will. I'll cut one from the thicket on the other hand, and then do you come out and fight. If you win, you'll have the hundred silver pounds. If I win, I'll take your brown cloak and your bow and arrows and your hunting-horn."

Then came the fiercest fight that ever a man did see. Two long hours of that bright summer's day it went on. At last Robin stumbled over the root of a tree and fell. Sir Guy struck him a terrible blow, and for a moment he lay as if dead. Then he sprang to his feet.

"A man must not die before his time," he cried; and he struck Sir Guy with a stroke so much heavier than his own that the man who would have shot him down like a wolf lay dead on the ground.

"I've heard of you of old, Sir Guy of Gisborne," said Robin. "You've ever been a traitor and a knave. Many's the true man you've brought to the gallows-tree. You've had the heavy strokes that you deserved long years ago, but I'll treat you kindly now, for I'll give you finer clothes than ever you bought with all the shillings and the pounds that the sheriff gave you, villain that has brought true men to death for the sake of the silver."

Then Robin put his cloak and tunic on Guy of Gisborne, and Sir Guy's brown cloak he hung over his own shoulders. Sir Guy's hunting-horn he hung by his side, and Sir Guy's bow and arrows he carried away in his hand as he went on the path that led to Bernisdale town.

"It's anxious that I am for my two good men that left me this morning," thought he, "and I've bethought me of a merry jest. I'll call out the proud sheriff and ask how they fare; and he himself shall show me the way to where they abide, for I'm sorely troubled lest William Scarlet and the wee bit laddie have come to harm."

When he came to the edge of the forest, Robin blew a loud and merry blast on the horn of Sir Guy. He blew another, and now he could see a great scampering to and fro in the market-place of Bernisdale town. Again he blew the horn, and went cheerily over the moor. Just outside the gates of Bernisdale, he met the sheriff and more than a score of men, all limping and stumbling.

"Welcome, great welcome," called the sheriff. "What news from the forest, Sir Guy?"

"Robin Hood and Guy of Gisborne had a fight," quoth Robin. "Under a tree lies a dead man, and he wears the green cloak and the green tunic of Robin Hood."

Then Robin hung Sir Guy's brown cloak over his own shoulders.

Then all the lame and bruised and ragged company set up a great shout of rejoicing.

"But what's the news in the town?" asked
Robin, "and why are there two gallows-trees set
up in the market-place?"

"By right, there should be three," said the
sheriff, "but William Scarlet slipped out of our
fingers, and we've only Little John left. He is
to be hanged on one. The second was built
for Robin Hood, but since he's dead, we'll just
leave it standing till we get another of the bold
outlaws."

They had come into the town, and across the
market-place Robin could see Little John fast
bound to the post of the gallows-tree.

"Hold your cloak, Sir Guy," called the sheriff,
"for here's the hundred silver pounds that I
promised to give to him that would take Robin
Hood."

"Thank you kindly," said Robin, "and, Master
Sheriff, should you think me too bold if I asked
one wee bit favor of you?"

"Ask what you will," replied the sheriff; and
Robin went on: —

"Now that I've slain the master, it would

give one great ease of mind if I could only strike one little blow on the knave that 's fast bound to the post; and this is the boon that I beg."

"Do what you will," said the sheriff, "but if you had asked of me double one hundred silver pounds, even if you had asked the fee of a belted knight, it should have been your own. It is n't every man that can take Robin Hood."

"No, Master Sheriff," answered Robin. "One should n't boast, but I 'd say humbly that no one caught Robin yesterday and no one will catch him to-morrow; and now I 'll strike my blow."

Then he went up to Little John, who was fast bound to the post of the gallows-tree. The sheriff and his men followed close after.

"Stand back, an it please you," cried Robin. "Give me room to swing my stout oaken staff. I 'll not kill the man. You can hang him afterwards."

But the blow that Robin struck was not with his stout oaken staff, but with his short, sharp knife, and it cut the rope that bound Little John.

Robin Hood: His Book

"Take this," said Robin; and Little John caught the bow of Sir Guy and fitted an arrow to the string.   The sheriff ran for his life, and so did all the sheriff's company, while Robin Hood and Little John sat under the gallows-tree and laughed to see them go.

XII

ROBIN GOES TO A WEDDING

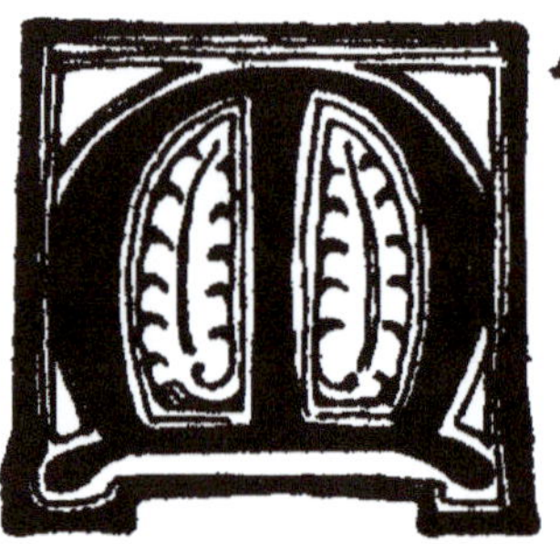

ASTER, Master," cried Little John, "there 's something a-coming down the lane under the beech-trees."

"It 's all in scarlet red," said Much the miller's son, "and it 's a-singing; and it 's dancing as if it could n't stay on its feet, it 's so glad. Master, what might it be ? "

"Mayhap it 's a knight, and his cloak 's lined with pieces of gold," suggested William Scarlet. "We 'll have him to dinner, Master."

"That 's no knight," said Robin; "he has no sword. Listen to what he sings." So they all stood still behind the trees, and the young man in scarlet red sang on at the top of his voice : —

"Heigh ho, the lassie, O !
To-morrow comes in the morning.
To-morrow day she 'll be my bride ;
To-morrow may no ill betide.
Heigh ho, the lassie, O !
To-morrow comes in the morning."

[176]

Little John went forward to the stranger. " My master gives you hearty greeting," said he, "and will you dine with us here in the good greenwood ? "

" That will I do and gladly," answered the young man in scarlet red.

" But have you any money to pay for the dinner ? " asked Little John.

" Money ? Yes, it 's plenty of money that I have," cried the young fellow eagerly. " See me count it. There 's one shilling for the feather-bed ; and there 's another for the kettle and the spoons ; and I can make the wooden bowl myself, I can, all out of the good beech-tree ; I 've made a bench already. And here 's a shilling left to buy a linsey-woolsey cloth to throw over it, for she 's not going to sit on a bench without a cushion, she 's not. And there 's a shilling to buy her a red ribbon when we go to the fair ; and there 's a shilling to give to the priest when he marries us. There 's many a man that 'll give the priest but a sixpence, and mayhap a crooked one at that, but I 'll give him a whole shilling, I will."

" Have you no goldpieces sewn in your scarlet cloak ? " asked Much the miller's son, "and have you no goldpieces sewn in your doublet ? "

" It 's gentlefolk that have goldpieces," answered the young fellow; " but yesterday I had another shilling, I did, and that makes six, it does, and that 's my wages for seven years' work. I paid one shilling for the ring; and now there 's one for the feather-bed, and another for the kettle and the spoons, and another for the cushion for the bench, and another for the priest, and another for the red ribbon, and that 's five shillings. It is n't every man that has five shillings to be married on. They all ring true, every one of them; and there 's one for the feather-bed, and another for the kettle and the spoons, and another for the cushion " —

" Master," whispered William Scarlet to Robin Hood, " let us go to the wedding."

" Be mannerly," said Robin. " There 's only one man that can ask leave to go to a wedding, and that 's the groom himself."

" Is it a wedding you 're talking of? " asked the young man. " The best wedding in the town will be to-morrow in the morning, at the little gray church on the hill, and I bid you one and all to come to it, for I 've one shilling for the priest, and another for the feather-bed, and another — "

" Thank you kindly," said Robin Hood. "We'll all come, and we'll have the wedding-feast under the beech-trees. But where are you going?" he cried, for the young man was making as if he would go away from the merry company. " Do you not mean to dine with us?"

" It's glad I'd be to stay with you," the young man called back over his shoulder, " but I have n't seen her since the early morning, and it might be that something has happened to her;" and down the lane he went, singing:—

> "Heigh ho, the lassie, O!
> To-morrow comes in the morning."

The next day Robin and his men made ready betimes to go to the wedding in the little gray church on the hill.

" When a man's going to meet the sheriff, it does n't matter which goes first," said Robin, " but if he's going to a wedding, he must be in the church before the bride comes in."

So they put on their best clothes, and every man stuck a new feather in his hat, and then they all set out merrily to go through the forest and across the moor and over the fence and up the hill to the little gray church; but before they came to the edge of the forest, they saw a young man whose clothes had been of the scarlet red, though now they were all draggled and torn. His sleeves were slit from the elbow to the wrist, and his hair stood out as many ways as there are winds that blow. His tunic hung down without a belt, his cloak dragged on the ground, and at every third step that he took, he moaned, " Alack and a-well-a-day."

" In faith, it 's our friend of the five shillings," said Robin, and he called out : —

" Friend, how goes it with the five shillings? Have you still one shilling for the feather-bed, and one for the red ribbon that you 'll buy at the fair? And were you so eager to see your guests that you left your bride to come out on the way to meet us ? "

" I 'm not to have any bride at all," groaned the young man, "for there was a knight of high degree that came for her, and her father says she shall marry him."

" And there was one shilling for the kettle and the spoons, and one shilling for the cushion for the bench, and one shilling for the feather-bed," murmured Much the miller's son.

Robin Hood: His Book

"Did you not fight for her?" asked Robin.

"No, Master," answered the young fellow simply, and a tear stood in either eye. "A knight of high degree would not fight with a man who had no sword, so I could only come away and leave him. I threw one of his servants over the hedge into the thorn patch, and another I swung across the limb of an oak, and another I rolled down the cliff into the sea, but I could n't do any fighting at all."

"That 's a pity," said Little John gravely, "for a bit of fighting will often make a man easier in his mind."

"How far away is the little gray church on the hill?" asked Robin.

"Only five miles," answered the young man with a groan.

Robin stood leaning on his bow while one could count ten. Then he said: —

"William Scarlet, do you take the young man and wash his face till it is red as a rose, and do you brush his hair till it shines like the sun on an ivy leaf."

Again Robin stood leaning on his bow, and this time one could count twenty. Then he said: —

Robin Hood: His Book

" Much the miller's son, do you take the young man and put on him a tunic and a mantle of fine woollen cloth, all of the scarlet red."

A third time Robin stood leaning on his bow, and now one could count thirty. Then he said:

" Little John, do you take the young man and hold him fast, and bring him after me through the forest and across the moor and over the fence and up the hill to the little gray church. I 've put on my best clothes to go to a wedding, and to a wedding I 'm going. If it is n't one, it shall be another; a man must n't be too particular."

" But, Master, what 'll you do for a bride and a groom ? " asked William Scarlet.

" There are girls all about the countryside as thick as daisies on a bank, and if there 's no groom, we 'll just take one of you. I 'll not put on my best clothes for nothing."

So through the forest and across the moor and over the fence went Robin. He was in his best clothes, but they were covered by a long green cloak, and a harp was swung around his neck by a green ribbon a full hand's breadth wide.

By and by he came to the little gray church on the hill.

Robin Hood : His Book

"Who is this," asked the bishop, "all in the green cloak, and with a harp hanging on a ribbon a full hand's breadth wide ?"

Then Robin bowed himself down to the ground.

"May it please your Reverence," said he, "I 'm a harper bold, and the best of all the harpers in the whole North Countree."

"What can you harp?" demanded the bishop.

"I can harp a tune that will make a man forget his bride and leave her at the altar; and I can harp another tune that will make a man five miles away hasten through the woods and across the moor and over the fence and up the hill till he comes to his own true love."

"You 're welcome," said the bishop right heartily. "Now give us a taste of your music."

"Never a string will I touch," declared Robin, "till the bride and the groom are on the threshold of the door of the church."

Then the door was opened wide, and in came the rich old knight. The hilt of his sword was red with rubies, the scabbard was green with emeralds, and a fringe of pearls was sewn all about his velvet mantle; but he leaned on a stout oaken staff, and his head shook with the palsy. He looked into the church, and then he frowned and called out angrily: —

"Where's the girl? Why isn't she here? I'll marry no girl that isn't here."

"You'll marry no girl that *is* here," said Robin to himself, for behind the old knight of high degree stood a pretty little village maiden. She had on a dress of heavy white satin, but it was much too large, for it had belonged to the knight's last two wives, and he would not buy a new dress for just one wedding. Round and round the neck of the maiden was twisted a long rope of diamonds and sapphires; but her blue eyes were bluer than the sapphires, and the tears that were falling from them were brighter than the diamonds.

"None of my wives ever kept me waiting before," grumbled the old knight.

"Get in with you, get in with you," whispered the father of the maiden, pushing her over the threshold. "Don't you know that a knight of high degree will not stand at the church door and wait for a village maiden?"

So the maiden with the blue eyes and the shining

tears was dragged into the church to be the bride of the old knight who was hobbling up to the altar.

"Now let the music begin," ordered the bishop.

"No man likes music better than I," said Robin, "but sometimes I like a harp, and sometimes I like a horn. This time we'll have the horn."

Then he drew out the hunting-horn from under his harper's cloak, and blew once, twice, and thrice.

Before the echo had died away, four and twenty good bowmen had come running through the forest and across the moor and over the fence and up the hill and into the little gray church. First of them all was Little John, and before him he pushed a young man whose face had been washed till it was red as a rose, and whose hair had been brushed till it shone like the sun on an ivy leaf, while his tunic and mantle were both of fine woollen cloth, all of the scarlet red.

The little village maiden turned pale for joy, the old knight turned red for anger, and the father called, "Go on, go on."

The bishop began : —

" Who giveth — " but he was so frightened that he forgot the rest of it, and stood with his mouth wide open like a great white owl on the tree-top, calling, " Who — who ? "

Then said Robin : —

" Little village maiden with the sapphire eyes and the diamond tears, will you be the bride of the knight of high degree and wear emeralds and pearls and rubies, or will you be the bride of the young man in the red cloak ? "

" I 'll marry no one but my own Allen à Dale," cried the little village maiden ; and she threw her white arms around the neck of the young man with the cloak of scarlet red.

The string broke, and the diamonds and sapphires rolled all over the church. Every one of them went into a mouse-hole, but the knight of high degree did not know it, and he got down on his knees and began to hunt.

" Why don't you go on and marry them ? " demanded Robin of the bishop; and the bishop answered nothing but " Who — who ? "

" The girl herself has told you ' who,' " shouted Robin. " It 's a poor bride that can't choose her own groom. Go on and marry her fast and firm to Allen à Dale."

"The bans must be cried three times," declared the bishop, "and I 'll not be the one to cry them."

"Come here, Little John," quoth Robin. "Let me see how good a bishop you will make."

So he pulled off the bishop's gown and put it on Little John. The bishop was short and Little John was tall, and the gown came only to Little John's waist.

"Never mind that," said Robin. "You 're the finest bishop I ever made in all my life."

Then Little John went up into the choir, and while the real bishop sat on the steps shivering with fear, Little John called the bans once, twice, and thrice.

"That 's not enough," said Robin. "Your gown is so short that you must talk longer."

Then Little John called the bans four, five, six, and seven times.

"That 'll do," said Robin. "Now marry the girl to Allen à Dale," he ordered the real bishop, and the bishop married them, but his voice trembled so that Robin made him say the words twice over for fear some of them had been left out.   When the bishop asked, " Who giveth this woman ? " Robin stepped up, and answered in a

voice that could be heard down the hill and over the fence and across the moor and through the forest : —

" I do, and the man that takes her from Allen à Dale shall pay for her dearly."

So it was that the little village maiden was married to her own true love, and then they all went away to the merry greenwood for a wedding feast, while the old knight of high degree stayed in the church and hunted in every corner to find the diamonds and sapphires that had all rolled down the mouse-hole.

XIII

ROBIN'S FRIEND, THE KNIGHT

OWN the highway rode the good knight, singing a merry little roundelay.

"Never did I meet a man so happy. You look as if you had seen the sun rise twice this morning." So said another good knight and true who came out of a crossroad.

"Greeting, old friend," cried the first. "If you had only been on this side the sea, I should not have been put to such straits for the four hundred pounds to save my lands."

"There's twice and three times four hundred pounds waiting for you in my treasure-room," said the second knight heartily.

"Well know I that, but my lands are safe now, I've had a visit with Robin Hood."

"It's not often that a knight comes away from Robin Hood richer than he went."

[190]

Robin Hood: His Book

"So long as I live I 'll be a friend to Robin," said the first knight, "for he 's freely given me the four hundred pounds to redeem my lands. I 'm on my way to the town of York and the Abbey of Saint Mary's, for there abides the stout abbot who lent me the money. If I be not there before to-morrow at vespers, there 'll be a feast and a rejoicing in the hall of the abbot, for then my land will be his own."

"My castle lies well on the way," said the second knight. " Let us go there and wait till to-morrow at sunrise, and then we 'll set out together to call on the stout abbot of Saint Mary's. I have a plan that will, it may be, give us no little of a jest."

The next day the abbot of Saint Mary's Abbey behaved as if he were mad. He ran from one door to another. He gazed up the hill and down the dale. He peered out of the loop-holes in the wall. He ran up the road a little way, and then he ran down the road. He was not used to so much exertion, and at last he dropped down heavily upon a wooden bench.

" Is there aught that one can do for you ? " asked a boy of the convent. " My master once told me a soothing drink that was good to heal all diseases; and he said if one put in saffron and tansy and stirred it with the right forefoot of a gray rabbit, it would even drive away evil spirits. Do evil spirits ever get into a great man, Sir Abbot?"

The abbot boxed the boy's ears, and they rang so that he thought all the bells of York were jingling. Then the abbot called for the prior.

"There's always trouble lying in wait for a man with a good heart," said he. "Now it's full twelve months that four hundred pounds of my money has been in the hands of the worthless knight that lives forty miles to the east of us. He was to bring it to-day, and he's not in sight."

"It's not yet noon," said the prior. "Mayhap he'll come before vespers."

"Yes, out of pure goodness I gave him till vespers," said the abbot. "I should have bidden him be here by sunrise."

"Have you no surety for the money?"

"Nothing more than his worthless lands."

"But his lands are worth five thousand pounds if they are a penny," exclaimed the prior.

"What's that to me?" cried the abbot. "He ought to have come before this hour of the day."

"He may be far beyond the ocean," said the prior. "He may be faint with hunger and stiff with cold. Who knows what mishaps befall those who fare beyond the seas. Will you not give him time to make his journey home?"

"You're ever against me," cried the abbot angrily. The high cellarer came in and the prior slipped out of the hall. The abbot would have been more angry than ever if he had known that the prior was going as fast as he could walk down the road by which the poor knight would be likely to come.

" A merry day to you, my Lord Abbot," said the high cellarer. " Have you forgotten that to-day the fat lands of the knight who dwells to the east of us will be your own?"

"But mayhap he'll come to pay the four hundred pounds," growled the abbot. "Luck is ever against me."

"Not he," returned the high cellarer cheerfully. "It's but a seven-night ago I had good tidings that he could not raise the four hundred pounds from friend or foe; and it's but two days since one in my pay saw him riding near the woods of Bernisdale."

"Little cause have we to wish Robin Hood good luck," said the abbot, "but if the knight is once in his hands, he'll not leave the forest with pound or with penny."

"Let us send for the lord high justice," suggested the high cellarer, "for it is before him that the knight will have to come, and we shall know all the sooner whether we have the rents from his broad lands for our own; and let us ask the sheriff to come, too, and then we'll have a feast."

They sent for the lord high justice and the sheriff, and then they talked about the merry days and nights that they would have with the rent from the broad lands of the knight.

All this time the good prior was hurrying down the road as fast as he could go, for he, too, was impatient to have a glimpse of the knight.

"If I could only see him and a true friend riding up the road," thought he, "and if they sang a cheery song, and the little bells on their bridle reins jingled in the breeze, then should I know that all was well with him."

Robin Hood: His Book

Not a bell and not a note of a cheery song did he hear, not even the beat of a horse's hoof on the well-trodden highway. Long he waited, but no one was in sight save two foot-farers who were coming slowly up a lane. Their clothes were old and dusty and stained and patched, and their eyes were downcast; but as they came near to the prior, he was sure that one of them was the knight whose broad lands lay to the eastward.

"Pardon me, good sir," said the prior to him who walked first in the narrow lane, — "pardon me, but might it be that you are the knight who holds the broad lands to the eastward?"

"Once held I broad lands," answered the knight sadly, "but to save my only son from the gallows-tree I pledged them all to the abbot, and they 're his own if I pay him not full four hundred pounds before the hour of vespers."

"And you have not the money?" asked the prior pityingly.

"Not a penny have I in my purse," declared the knight; and he pulled out a faded silken purse.

"Then why do you come to the abbot if you 've no money in your purse?" asked the prior.

Robin Hood: His Book

"Sometimes a rich man of good heart will grant a bit longer time rather than see a true knight become a beggar," said he. "Think you that he will show me the favor?"

"If you could but give him a part of the money, he might," answered the prior doubtfully. "The sight of goldpieces will sometimes make a man do what he thought he would not."

"It looks as if there was little hope for me then," said the knight, and again he shook his empty purse. "Shall we turn back?" he asked of his friend; but the prior called : —

"Stay — it might be — a man should try — would you take it amiss if — I've but one hundred pounds — will you take it and see if the abbot will grant you time?"

The knight looked at his friend, and his friend looked at the knight. Then said the knight : —

"I did not think there were three men in England with so good a heart as yours. I will pluck up courage and go to the stout abbot, and if I can save my lands, you shall not be the loser." There were tears in his eyes as he spoke, but the prior looked as happy as if some one had just given him a hundred pounds. He went around by a little lane and crept into the abbey by a postern gate; but the knight and his friend walked boldly up to the great door of the hall and knocked as loud as if they each of them had four hundred pounds in his pocket.

"Rap, rap, rap," sounded on the door. The lord high justice and the high cellarer and the sheriff and the stout abbot had decided, as the hour for vespers drew near, that the knight would not come. They were having a fine feast all by themselves at the table in the great hall, and were in the midst of such an uproarious time that they did not hear even the loud knock on the door.

"We'll do better than this to-morrow night," cried the stout abbot, "and we'll have a feast every night for a year."

"Those broad lands are worth full six thousand pounds," said the high cellarer.

"And I'll declare them yours," quoth the lord high justice, "if he should come but the wink of an eye beyond his time. I'll not take a man's robe and fee and not stand by him, I won't."

"It's not a half-hour to vespers," declared the stout abbot, looking at the sun-dial.

Robin Hood: His Book

"Rap, rap, rap," sounded again on the great door, and this time the abbot heard it. He looked first white and then red. He half rose from his seat, and then he sank down again.

Meanwhile the high cellarer had slipped up the stairs and looked out through the loophole in the wall. He came running down in great delight.

"It's he, it's he," he cried, "but his clothes are dusty and ragged and stained and patched, and the friend that's with him looks even worse. He has no money."

Then the stout abbot took courage and opened the great hall door, but not a word of welcome did he speak. The two knights entered the room, and gave courteous greeting, first to the abbot, then to the lord high justice, then to the sheriff, and then to the high cellarer. The knight bent on one knee before the stout abbot.

"Sir Abbot," said he, "it may well be that a great man like you has forgotten the debt of four hundred pounds that I owe you."

"Have you brought your money?" growled the abbot.

Have you brought your money!
growled the Abbot of St Marys.

"Alas, I've not a penny in my purse," said the knight, holding forth the empty purse, "but —"

"There's no 'but' about it," thundered the abbot. "What are you here for? Go on with the feast. Drink to my health, Sir Justice."

"But, Sir Abbot," pleaded the knight, "to save a true knight from poverty, will you not give me but a little longer time?"

"Never a day," shouted the stout abbot.

"Good Sir Justice," begged the knight, "will you not be my friend? Will you not see right done me?"

"By robe and fee," declared the lord high justice, "I am bound to the abbot."

"Good Sir Sheriff," pleaded the knight, "will you not beg the abbot to give me but a single month to save my lands?"

"It's not my business to help good-for-naughts out of their scrapes," said the sheriff, "it's my business to hang them."

"Sir High Cellarer," begged the knight, "I had a good friend and true, but when I went to his castle a seven-night ago, he was still over the seas. He would have given me four hundred pounds and thrice four hundred. Will you not beg the abbot to give me the time to go once more to his castle and see if he has not yet returned ? "

" I won't give you another minute," shouted the stout abbot. "You have n't the gold, and you can't get it before vespers. Go out of my hall, false knight as you are."

Then rose the knight from his knee and strode up the room.

" A truer knight than I never lived," said he. " Never has knight been braver in joust or tournament, never has one pressed more boldly into the fray. Debtor as I am, I tell you, Sir Abbot, here in your own hall, that the words you have spoken are lying words. You have no truth, and you have no courtesy. None but a boor would suffer a knight to kneel so long before him."

The stout abbot began to be afraid. " What shall I do ? " he whispered to the lord high justice; and the lord high justice whispered back :

" Offer him one hundred pounds to agree that you shall hold the land in peace." So the stout abbot offered the knight one hundred pounds. The knight shook his head.

"Offer him two hundred," whispered the lord high justice, "and make him promise to cross the seas."

The knight said a few words in the ear of his friend. Then they turned toward a round table that stood in the corner of the hall. From under his ragged cloak the friend drew out a leathern bag. He shook it, and as he shook, one goldpiece after another fell out, until there lay on the table full four hundred pounds.

"Here is your gold, Sir Abbot," said the knight, "and here is one hundred pounds more that I should have given you, had you been kindly and courteous."

The abbot's head fell over on his shoulder. He looked at the lord high justice, and the lord high justice looked at him. Then the knight and his friend went out of the great door of the hall singing a merry little song; and as they came to the turn of the road, there stood the good prior under an oak-tree, waiting to see them.

"One needs but a look at your faces," said he, "to see that it has gone well with you. A simple prior must say naught against his abbot, but I feared sorely that your way would be hard."

Robin Hood: His Book

"What should you say," asked the knight, jestingly, "if you saw me going away with one hundred pounds that I did not bring?"

The prior meekly crossed himself:—

"The saints have softened his heart," said he, "or else"—and here he crossed himself again hastily and half fearfully—"it might be that evil spirits have entered into him and that he will go mad."

"Let the great churchmen settle it," said the knight with a laugh, "but here's the hundred pounds that you lent me, and I'll warrant you the saints had more to do with that than the fiends. Here's another hundred to go with it, Sir Prior; and if ever you want a friend for yourself or any of your kin, come you by night or by day, by Sunday or by Monday, by moonlight or by sunlight, there's a man dwelling forty miles to the eastward who'll do for you as he would for his own brother;" and while the good prior looked first at the gold and then at the knight, the knight and his friend went down the lane and sprang upon their horses that waited for them behind the hedge and rode gayly off to the friend's castle.

Robin Hood: His Book

Then the knight took off his worn and ragged and dusty clothes and put on a blue satin tunic and a crimson velvet mantle. He put rings on his fingers, a gold chain around his neck, a hat with a long white feather on his head, and off he went to tell his wife all about it.

The gate of his castle was open, and the portcullis was up. His wife stood weeping by the door of the keep.

"Alas and alas," she sobbed, "I know all that you can say to me. The land is lost, and we must go out into the world and beg our bread."

"There's always some little thing that a woman does n't know, and it's often and often the thing that she thinks she knows best," cried the knight gayly.

Then he sat down beside her and held her hand in his, and told her how he had gone to his friend's castle and found that his friend was over the seas; then how he had gone through Bernisdale, not knowing where he was, and not caring. When he came to tell her that Robin Hood's men had captured him, but that when they found in what pitiful trouble he was, they had feasted him and given him a horse and a mantle and four hundred pounds in gold that he might win back his lands, then his good wife started up.

"Not another word," said she, "till I've been in the chapel and said a prayer for Robin Hood and every one of his good men."

It was not many months before the knight made ready to pay a visit to Robin Hood. He had one hundred bows made of the finest yew, all rubbed and polished till they shone like the moon on a lake, and the strength of every bow was tried with care by the strongest man on all his lands. With every bow there was a sheaf of arrows, and every arrow was a full ell in length. The arrow-heads were burnished so bright that when one was shot, it looked like a moonbeam flashing its way through the air. Nor were these arrows winged with the quill of the goose, for every one of them was gleaming and glittering in the sunlight with a peacock's feather of green and gold, bound fast to the head of the shaft by a ring of silver.

When the bows and arrows were all together, it was a beautiful sight; and when the knight put beside them four hundred pounds in gold, every piece of which had been rubbed and rubbed until he could see his own face in it as well as the king's, the knight's wife clapped her hands for pleasure.

" No one but myself shall knit the purse for the golden coin," said she; and soon she had knit a silken purse with her own white fingers.

Then the good knight brought together one hundred of his strongest and bravest followers, and they set out to carry to Robin Hood the shining gold and the bows of the good yew-tree, and the arrows that were winged with peacock feathers.

It was a splendid sight.   First came the knight on a great black charger.   He wore a white tunic and a scarlet cloak and a gold chain, and he carried a javelin.   Behind him was a stout man all in black, riding a white horse.   Across the saddle in front of him lay the silken purse that had been knit by the lady of the castle, and through its meshes shone the four hundred pieces of gold. Then came the hundred followers of the knight, each one on a good roan steed, and each one wearing a blue tunic and a white cloak.   Every man carried a yew-tree bow, and a sheaf of the arrows that were winged with the feathers of the peacock.

The morning was fresh and fair, and the sun shone down on the silver arrow-heads and the polished bows, and they flashed back at the sun. Down the road the horsemen went, and as they galloped on, they sang a lightsome song.

There was a bridge that lay in their way, and just beyond it was an open field. As they drew near, they could see that the games of the country were going on. Most of the men wore the dress of countrymen, but there was one whose garb was different. As the knight looked at him, he thought, "Where is it that I have met that face? I wish I might see him without his hood."

At one side under a tree were the prizes. There was a white bull, and near it stood a handsome black horse, all saddled and bridled. The saddle was tipped with silver, and the bridle shone with gold. There was, too, a pair of gloves with finely wrought gauntlets, a pipe of wine, and a ring of red, red gold.

"Those be rarely handsome prizes for a wrestling," said one of the men-at-arms to the knight.

"True," agreed the knight. "We will bide

awhile and see the match. No one will note that we be here over this little hill. The stranger yonder seems to me the best of them. The folk hereabouts do not like strangers, and if he wins, they may treat him roughly. We'll stay and see to it that he has whatever prize he earns."

So the knight and his hundred men-at-arms sat on their horses and watched the games go on. First there was a running match, whose prize was the great white bull; and the stranger won the bull. Next came a leaping match, whose prize was the handsome black horse all saddled and bridled; and the stranger won the horse. Then came a lifting match. The one who could lift most was to have the pipe of wine; and the stranger won the pipe of wine. The next trial was to throw a heavy stone. The one that could throw it farthest was to have the pair of gloves with finely wrought gauntlets; and the stranger won the gloves.

All this time the countrymen were looking more and more angry. They began to gather in little groups and to glance sullenly at the stranger. The knight and his men were watching closely.

"I fear me there 'll be trouble," said the knight, "if the stranger takes the last prize. Let us go a bit nearer."

The crier stepped forward and called: —

"A ring, a ring, a ring of red, red gold, and it is to go to him who shall throw the man that was the champion at the last match."

Then a stout, burly man came forward, brandishing his fists. He stepped up to the stranger and called him out to a combat. All the men around stopped talking to one another and gazed at the stranger and the champion. Nearer came softly the knight and his men.

"I 've no wish to wrestle," said the stranger.

"Wrestle you shall," declared the champion.

"No man need try for a prize against his will," declared the stranger.

"You 'll not go free against *my* will," growled the champion. "No man comes here and takes the prizes that belong to us without paying for them."

So saying, he struck the stranger a heavy blow. The knight started forward, then stopped.

"The man can hold his own," thought he; and he and his hundred men sat on their horses and watched.   Soon they saw that not the champion, but the stranger was getting the best of it.   The countrymen saw this, too, and just as the stranger was about to strike a blow that would have thrown the champion, a stout country fellow rushed forward with his fists doubled up, all ready to attack the stranger.

"Two against one," cried the good knight. "That's no fair play."   He galloped down to the field and thrust his javelin between the two men.

"Who gave the prizes for these games?" he demanded.

"These be the king's prizes," answered the chief of the games.

"May not any one try for them who will?"

"I suppose so," answered the chief sullenly.

"The stranger won every prize," said the knight, "and what is more, he shall have them."   He waved his hand, and all the hundred knights came riding down the little hill, and took their stand about the stranger, while the countrymen went glumly away, giving many a surly look at the winner of the prizes.

"If you will mount the handsome black horse," said the knight to the stranger, "one of my men

will lead the white bull, another shall bear the pair
of gloves and the ring of red, red gold, another
the pipe of wine, and we will go with you wherever you say. It might be that some of those
men would try to work you harm. There's one
who was good to me while I was in need, and for
his sake I'll see no harm done to an honest
stranger."

"And who might that be?"

"Robin Hood," answered the knight.

"It's not often that a knight speaks well of
Robin," said the stranger.

"There's one knight that will never let the
chance go by to do him a favor. But do you
point out the way that you would take, and we
will see to it that you have a safe journey whither-
soever you wish to go."

The stranger pointed toward the wood, and
into the forest they went. The shade grew more
and more dense. Then there was a half-open
space where the sun flickered down gayly through
the branches.

"This looks much like the place where I met
my kind friend, Robin Hood," said the knight;
and even as he spoke, one good bowman and then

another came into view, until the wood seemed to be full of them.

"Surely, these be Robin Hood's men," said the knight joyfully, for he remembered more than one face that had bent toward him kindly when he was in dire distress.

The stranger threw back his hood, and behold, it was Robin himself.

XIV

ROBIN MEETS HIS MATCH

AR up in the North Countree was a fair maiden, and it was of her that Robin was dreaming all one bright summer day. At last he said to his good men : —

" I think I 'll walk a bit."

" Shall I not go with you, Master Robin? " asked George à Green.

" No, thank you kindly, man. I 'd best be alone awhile."

Robin walked fast and far. No thought had he where he was going, and while he was still dreaming of the fair maiden, he found himself on the highway and face to face with a sturdy beggarman.

The beggarman wore a long cloak, and wherever it had grown threadbare, it had been patched,

[212]

until the very thinnest place in it was full twenty-fold thick, and it was of all the colors that the sun ever shone upon. On the beggarman's head he wore a hat; on that was another hat, and on the second was yet another. One hat was brown, and one was green, and one was red. The red one was on top, and in the pointed crown was stuck a long, black cock's feather. Many a bag, both large and small, dangled from his belt. About his neck was a broad strap fastened by a stout buckle, and from the strap hung a leathern pouch to hold the meal that he begged. In his hand was a heavy pike-staff. The upper part was wood, and the lower part was iron. Never was a man better guarded from harm, be his foes wind and weather, or be they only of the human kind.

"Give me a shilling," demanded the beggar, thrusting his fist full into Robin's face. No man was ever more kind to the poor than Robin, but to have a vision of the fairest maid of the North Countree driven away by the dirty fist of a beggar angered him well.

"I'll not," said he; and he lifted up his staff to strike. The beggar ran.

"Come back here," called Robin.

"Not I," said the beggar. "It's the time for supper, and I should look foolish, indeed, walking into mine inn when the supper hour's long past."

"You're not over thin," said Robin. "You've had your dinner surely."

"What's that to you?" demanded the beggar.

"Naught but this," quoth Robin. "You've had your dinner as well as I. Now you would have your supper, and you've no care for mine. Will you lend me a shilling for my supper?"

"I've no money to lend," retorted the other. "You're no true beggarman. Where are your bags, if you are a beggar? Where is your well-patched cloak? I believe you're naught but an outlaw, and I'd have little wonder, indeed, if you were Robin Hood himself."

"Whoever I am," cried Robin, "you're to lend me the money for a supper; and if you do it not, I'll have it from those bags of yours. Loosen the strings, and quickly now, or, in faith, I'll open every one of them with my own good knife; and what's more, I'll find out whether an arrow will make its way through the tough skin of a beggar-man."

Robin Hood: His Book

The beggar laughed loud and long and came a step nearer.

"So you think you'll frighten me with your silly chatter, do you? Little care I for your knife or for the pointed sticks that you've stuck into your belt. The man that fights me would do well to look for better weapons than those pudding-sticks of yours."

Robin fitted an arrow to his bow, and he would soon have known whether it would pierce a beggar's skin had not the stout beggarman suddenly whirled about, and struck such a blow with his iron pike-staff that the bow fell into two pieces; and as for the arrows, they looked more like a well-stirred pudding than like pudding-sticks.

Robin drew his sword, but another terrible blow from the iron pike-staff broke the weapon, and wounded his wrist so that if he had had a hundred swords, not one of them could he have drawn. Now he was helpless, and the blows came heavy and fast. His face was white, his eyes were closed, and he fell on the ground in a swoon.

"Get up, get up!" cried the beggarman. "Shame on you for going to bed before the sun has set! Stand up and take my money if you will, and then you can go boldly to the tavern, and you can say, ' Give me wine and give me ale. Here's the money I borrowed from a simple beggarman on the highway, and that 'll pay the score.' Go on, man. If you stay by yourself so long, your friends will laugh at you and say you 're dull as a beetle. Stand up and be a man."

Robin lay still as a stone. The beggarman laughed a loud, mocking laugh, and then strode down the highway. He gave one look back and called jeeringly : —

" Next time you 'd best see what a man's staff is shod with before you go a-begging of him."

Three of Robin's good men were talking together long after their master had gone on his walk.

" It 's two good hours since Master Robin went away," said one.

" He 's safe enough," said another. " He knows how to make his way. He can get the better of any man."

" There 's hardly one of our good company that could not get the better of him in a fair fight," said the third, "but somehow he makes us all feel as if he were the stronger."

"I'm going a bit along the way he went," declared the first, and the others followed.

When they came to the highway, what should they see but Robin lying on the ground. His face was pale, his eyes were closed, and he was faintly making a low and piteous moan.

"Master, Master," they called, but there came no answer save this sad and grievous moaning. They brought water and cast upon his face, and at last he opened his eyes. No wound could they see, but the red blood was trickling from between his lips. By and by he could sit up, and then he told the whole sorry tale.

"Do one of you stay with me," he bade, "lest I breathe my last breath here by the way alone; and let the other two go over hill and over dale and find the evil beggarman. It was no fair fight, it was murder. Bring him back and let him be punished for his crimes. And see that you give him no chance to wield that iron staff of his, for whether you be one or two or three, I fear he'll be too much for you."

"Think you, Master Robin, that two of your

men can be beaten by a low-born beggarman with a twig ? " asked one.

" We 'll soon bind him fast and well," declared another, " and he shall stand here and be tied to this tree, and we will ask, ' Master Robin, what is your will? Shall he be slain, or shall he be hanged high, high, on a great oak-tree? ' and whatever thing you say, that thing will we do."

" Be wary, be wary," bade Robin with a groan. " Grasp firm hold of the terrible pike-staff. Go up behind him by stealth, and see that you give him no chance for one single blow."

" We 'll be sure of him. Farewell, Master, farewell," they cried; and one looked back over his shoulder to call, " Don't forget, Master, to be a-thinking whether you 'd rather have him hanged or slain."

The bold beggarman strolled on up the hill and then down the hill. He walked as slowly as if there was no fear of being overtaken, and as rapidly as if there was no chance that two stout men might be waiting for him at the turn of the road. It was sure to be one thing or the other, for Robin's two men had set out with good hearts and brave to right their master's wrongs.

Robin Hood: His Book

On stalked the beggar, and when he reached the top of the hill, he stopped a minute in the breeze. He lifted off one hat and then another. Then he threw aside his well-patched cloak and stretched his arms back and yawned comfortably.

Robin's two men saw him standing on the hilltop. He was two miles away, but they knew well a little crossroad that ran through the fields and saved a full mile. The beggar sauntered on in the highway, but Robin's men ran with all their might. They sank in the mire, they waded through the dark pools, they dashed up hill, and they stumbled down hill. Neither high nor low could keep them, and a full half-hour before the beggar came, they were in a little wood in a dark glen, well hidden, each behind a tree, one on one side of the road and one on the other.

The beggar came up whistling " A jolly pinder of Wakefield." No thought had he of what was to come, and no care had he for the ill that he had wrought. He was swinging the iron-bound pike-staff in time with his whistling, and as he came to the two trees he struck one of them to mark the end of his verse.

Behind the tree stood George à Green, and before the pike-staff could be swung back, he had seized it by the iron end. With one fierce thrust, he tumbled the sturdy beggar upon the ground, and before the fellow could stir hand or foot, Friar Tuck was standing over him with a sharp knife.

Never was there a more frightened man than the sturdy beggar. His pike-staff was gone, and the point of the sharp knife was at his heart.

" Give me my life," he pleaded. " I 've done naught to you or yours. Why would you slay a simple beggar who goes to and fro in the hard world, begging his bread from door to door? You 'll win little of honor and little of fame by the death of a poor beggarman."

Not a word had Robin's men spoken, but now Friar Tuck said : —

" You 've all but killed the gentlest master and the truest friend that ever a man had. We 'll bind you fast and well, and we 'll drag you through briar and brake, up hill and down dale, till we come to Master Robin, and then you shall be slain or hanged on the highest tree in the forest, as he shall say, if only he be alive to speak to us."

Then thought the sturdy beggarman, " They have my pike-staff, and the knife is at my heart. Naught can I do against the strength of two stout men ; " so he pleaded : —

" Brave gentlemen, what will it boot you to spill the blood of a beggar ? I did but in my own defence what I was forced to do. May not a man defend himself when he is set upon by another ? I pray you let me go, and I will make you such a gift as you have not had for many a day. I 've a hundred pounds of gold and I 've much silver all hidden away. Give me your word to let me go, and you shall have the silver and the gold."

" He can't run away from us," whispered one of the men to the other. " Little doubt have I that the gold 's hid in that clouted cloak of his. It 's as thick as a feather-bed, and we never could find the money. Let us say to him that if the gold is as much as he says, we will take it, and we will agree not to drag him back to Master Robin to be hanged. He 'll count it out fast enough if he thinks he can save his life; and we 'll be speaking true, for we 'll not drag him back to Master Robin, but we 'll hang him here to yonder good stout oak-tree."

"I doubt whether Master Robin would be pleased if we take the man's life after we 've taken the gold," said the other thoughtfully.

"We 'll put the gold into the treasure-box, and Master Robin need know nor word nor lisp of it," said the first. "The fellow's a knave, and it's good to get all out of him that we can. Naught is it to Master Robin whether the rascal's hanged before his eyes or here on yonder oak."

Then said they to the beggarman: —

"False carl that you are, all the gold and all the silver that your clouted cloak would hold is but a small fee for what you have done to our good master; but count out your gold, and if so be that it is as much as you say, then will we agree that you shall not be dragged back to him to be hanged."

"Thank you, kind sirs, thank you," said the beggar humbly. "I 'll lay down my cloak, and on it I 'll count out my silver and my gold. It's all that I 've saved for many a long year."

"Be quick about it then," bade Friar Tuck.

Robin Hood: His Book

The beggar spread out his heavy cloak. He
was careful to put it between them and the wind,
for he had a little plan in his mind and he was not
so cast down as he seemed. Slowly and carefully
he unbuckled the strap and took off the leathern
meal-bag.

"Have patience, kind sirs," he pleaded. "The
gold's safely hidden away in the bottom of my
bag; but we'll soon be to it. Have patience."

Robin's men were more used to fearless fighting than to patient waiting, and as the beggar
slowly poured the meal out upon the clouted
cloak, they called : —

"Hasten, hasten. Do you think we've naught
to do but to stand here and see you pour out
meal?"

"Good sirs, I must lose my gold, but surely
you would not make a poor beggar lose the bit
meal that he has gathered, a handful at a time,
from door to door? But, Masters, I could pour
it faster if you would be so good as to hold down
the corners of the cloak."

George à Green and Friar Tuck each knelt on
one knee and held a corner of the cloak. The
beggar opened the bag wide, and the meal fell in

a great heap. The bowmen looked eagerly to see the gold tumble, but all in a moment the sturdy beggar caught a handful of meal in either hand and flung it straight into their faces; and before they could spring upon their feet, he had shaken the cloak over their heads. Not a word could they say, for their mouths were full; and not a ray of light could they see, for their eyes were full. It was all they could do to breathe.

Now the sturdy beggarman grasped his iron pike-staff again and struck about him lustily. "Your pardon, Masters, your pardon," he cried merrily. "A humble beggarman should have had more care of the clothes of his betters. Indeed, sirs, pardon me but this once, and I will gladly do all that I can to make it right. Good meal harms no one, and with my own true pike-staff I will beat it off for you, and I will spare neither labor nor pains."

Indeed, he spared no labor, but as for the pains, they belonged to George à Green and Friar Tuck, for on each of them fell at least a dozen sound blows from the terrible pike-staff.

As soon as they could see but a wee glimmering of light, away they ran for their very lives, while the beggarman stood leaning on his staff and roaring with laughter.

"Come back, come back," he cried. "Truly, it grieves me sorely that I should have wasted good meal on those clothes of yours. Come back, and give a poor beggarman a chance to get it again. And you 've not yet been paid your gold. Come back and see what 's in the bottom of the bag."

The more he called, the faster they ran, and ever they could hear behind them the hoarse chuckle of the beggarman and his cry, "Come back, come back."

When the meal was wiped out of their eyes, they would willingly have pursued the beggar to the world's end, but deep into the thick wood had he fled, and the night was so near that one could have found neither friend nor foe in the darkness. Home they went, two as shamefaced bowmen as ever roamed the forest.

"And where is the beggarman?" cried Robin. "Here are trees enough, but there 's no man to hang on them." George à Green and Friar Tuck only hung their heads in shame.

"You 've been at the mill, lads?" asked Robin.

"No, Master," answered they.

"But look at your clothes," said Robin; and the other bowmen gathered closely about and pointed their fingers and whispered, "Look at them, look at them."

Lower hung the heads of the abashed avengers, and the two men dropped to the ground without a word. Then said Robin:—

"Never had I so faithful followers before. You fight with me, and more than that, you even swoon with me. But tell me now what it is that has befallen you?"

The two men told the whole story, and then said Robin:—

"Indeed, one must be ready to take what he is ready to give, and it might be that I did wrong to try to win a bit of silver from a man who was neither knight nor sheriff nor bishop. Have your supper, laddies, and go you to rest. There's a fine bit of venison on roasting for you—" and then Robin really couldn't help adding slyly, "unless it might be that you like better a well-baked cake of the fine-sifted meal."

XV

ROBIN AND THE MONK

T was the morning of Whitsunday, and all was fresh and fair in the forest. The birds were singing, the little flowers were blooming, and even the green leaves gleamed and shone in the bright May sunshine. Robin stood leaning against a tree.

"Master, what are you —" began Much the miller's son; but William Scarlet whispered : —

"Hist! Don't talk to him. When a man's thinking, he may be going to do something."

"Little John," said Robin, "it 's full two weeks since I 've been in the church. Whoever is a true man ought to hear a mass on Whitsunday. Can you say whether the proud sheriff is at home?"

"He 's not, Master," answered Little John. "He 's gone full thirteen miles away to eat his Whitsunday dinner with his cousin."

Robin Hood: His Book

"Then will I go to the church," declared Robin.

"Take twelve good bowmen with you," pleaded William Scarlet.

"No, I'll go alone," said Robin. "When one goes to hear mass, he must not be thinking of bowmen."

So through the woods Robin went on his way to hear mass at Nottingham. The gate-keeper came out to greet him. "I'm a sworn man," said he, "that I'll never see Robin Hood go through my gates alive, so while I shut my eyes, sir, do you just slip into the town."

Robin went safely through the town gates and into the church, and knelt down before the great cross; and there he counted his beads and said a prayer for himself, and began to say another for each one of his men. The sun rose higher and higher, and people came into the church; but not one of them did Robin see, for he had not yet said prayers enough for half of his followers. Many a man was looking at him, and one whispered to another : —

"It's he, and he sent my wife a bit of venison when she was sick ; " and another whispered : —

" He dropped a silver shilling over my shoulder when I was ploughing."

A woman said to her neighbor: —

" It 's our own Master Robin, and he gave me the very cloak I have on; " and the neighbor whispered : —

" He gave my daughter one hundred pounds for a dowry. He took it away from the great-headed monk, and the monks were going to make a feast with it, and they all vowed they 'd have his life."

The parish priest was at the altar, and when he turned to the people, he too saw Robin. He looked about anxiously lest the sheriff should be in sight.

" It 's Robin that gave me the money to buy the lame woman a pig when the sheriff took the only one she had; and it 's Robin that gave my poor mother a cow when hers was drowned in the bog," thought the parish priest. " May all the saints preserve him ! "

So said the priest, and so said the people, but now the door swung wide open, and the great-headed monk strode in. He strutted up the aisle with his head held high, and his arms swinging so that the people who were kneeling scrambled to their feet to get out of his way. When he was half-way up to the altar, he suddenly stopped, then he turned and ran out of the door. Not a bit of this had Robin seen, for he had not yet finished saying a prayer for each one of his men.

The great-headed monk hurried to the city gates, and bade that they be shut fast and barred and bolted. Then he ran full thirteen miles to the cousin's house where the sheriff had gone to eat his Whitsunday dinner. Never had the great-headed monk run so fast or so far.

The sheriff and his wife sat at the cousin's table. The sheriff was just taking his first glass of wine when he heard a noise.

" What 's that? " he cried.

" That 's naught but the cook opening the oven door," answered the cousin — and all the time it was really the great-headed monk stumbling on the front doorstep.

In a minute there was another noise.

" What 's that? " cried the sheriff.

" That 's naught but the cook drawing the big pudding out of the oven," answered the cousin —

and all the time it was really the great-headed monk fumbling with the big brass knocker on the front door.

In a minute there was another noise.

" What's — " began the sheriff, but he did not finish, for the great-headed monk burst into the room and called : —

" O Sheriff, Sheriff, come with me. There's a felon and knave in the church at Nottingham."

" Never a step will I go," said the sheriff, "till I 've had one, two, and three glasses of good red wine."

" But it 's the king's felon," shouted the monk full in his ear as if he were deaf.

" The king has felons in plenty," said the sheriff calmly, " and I 've not often such wine as this.   I 'll not lose it for all of them."

" But it 'll be your fault if he gets away," shrieked the monk. " He stole one hundred silver pounds from me, and he 's at the mass."

" Then he 's doing no harm," retorted the sheriff, "and I 'll go for him when I 've had my three glasses of wine."

" But it 's Robin Hood," screamed the monk.

" Simpleton that you are, why did n't you say so ? " roared the sheriff.

The wine-bottle flew one way and the wooden stool another. The table gave a great lurch, and while the cousin and the cousin's wife and the sheriff's wife were trying to save all the good things from falling down among the rushes, the sheriff ran out of the door and down the steps. He thought that he caught up his cap and mantle as he ran. It was really his wife's purple hood

and scarlet cloak, but he did not know it; and
down the road he tore with the scarlet cloak
flying out in the wind and the purple hood hanging over one shoulder. After him came the
great-headed monk, crying out: —

"Hasten, Master Sheriff, hasten, or he'll be
gone, and he stole one hundred silver pounds
from me, he did."

They ran all the thirteen miles to Nottingham.
Then the sheriff went through the gate, and
called out two-score men to go with him to take
Robin Hood. They dashed in at the church
door, and just as Robin finished his prayer for
the last one of his men, his enemies surrounded
him with clubs and stones and sticks and cudgels
and bludgeons, and any other kind of weapon that
they had been able to snatch in their hurry.

"Would that only one of my good men were
with me," thought Robin. He drew out his two-
handed sword that hung down by his knee, and
where the crowd was thickest, he began to strike.
One and another fell till twelve of them lay dead
on the church floor. A terrible blow did Robin
give full on the sheriff's head, but now in the
time when he had most need of it, the good sword

failed. In the twinkling of an eye it was in two pieces, and lay on the stone floor that was slippery with the blood of the twelve men.

So it was that Robin was taken prisoner. He was bound with three stout ropes, each tied in seven twisted knots, and then all the company set out for the jail. The sheriff went first, with the purple hood and the scarlet cloak. Then came Robin Hood, bound with the three stout ropes, and each of them tied in seven twisted knots. On either side of Robin were two strong men with their two sharp swords, and behind Robin walked four others, and each of these had a pike in his hand. They marched off to the stone jail, and the sheriff knocked on the door.

" Who is there ? " called the jailer.

" The sheriff of Nottingham, and here is the worst felon in the land. He 's bound with three stout ropes, and every rope is tied in seven twisted knots. Take him, and see that you lock him into the lowest dungeon cell of the whole jail."

Then was Robin put into the lowest dungeon cell of the whole jail, and his door was locked fast and barred and bolted.

" Be sure you bolt the outer door," cried the sheriff, as they went away. " Those men of his are worse than thieves, and they 'll break in and set him free. See to it that you let no man in unless I bring him."

" Be sure you bolt the prison gate," called the great-headed monk. " He robbed me of one hundred silver pounds once, he did."

Then said the sheriff: —

" Now will I write a letter to the king, and I 'll send it by a trusty man, and it 'll say : ' The bold outlaw Robin Hood is fast in the prison of Nottingham town. He 'll not get away, for it 's the sheriff that 's watching him, and the sheriff knows how to hold on to a rascal. No one slips through his fingers.' "

" I 'll gladly bear the letter myself," said the great-headed monk, " for he robbed me of one hundred silver pounds."

The letter was written and given to the monk. He set out with a page for the king's court. The sheriff went with him as far as the town gate, and he bade the gate-keeper: —

" See to it that you lock the gates well this night, for the bold outlaw Robin Hood is down

in the lowest dungeon cell of the prison, and he 'll
either break out or the knaves that follow him
will come to his rescue."

Then said the sheriff to his men: —

" Get your bows ready and your axes and your
knives and your swords, for Robin Hood will
try to get out before sunrise. A sheriff has to
be awake. Other men may shut their eyes, but
mine have to be wide open. Nobody will get
into the prison unless I bring him "—and here
the sheriff threw back his head with a loud laugh
— " but Robin will try to get out, and you must
be ready for him."

Over the good greenwood the sun rose higher
and higher until it peered straight down through
the tops of the trees.

" It is time for Master Robin to be here," said
William Scarlet.

" He 's not the man to come out at the church
door till he 's said a prayer for every one of us,"
said Much the miller's son.

Then said Little John: —

" The sun begins to go down over the trees,
Let us take off our green cloaks and our hunting

caps with the feathers, and let us go out on the highway to seek for tidings."

So they took off their green cloaks and their caps with the feather in each, and they went out on the highway to seek for tidings of Robin.

Before long a monk came riding by on a fine gray horse, and behind him rode a page. Low louted the three men before him, and William Scarlet said : —

"A humble greeting to you, sir. Is there any news from Nottingham ?"

"I 've no time to chatter with folk like you," replied the great-headed monk, for it was he himself on his way to the king's court. "I 've a letter to bear to the king."

"It 's only a man of mark that 's trusted with a letter to the king," murmured Much the miller's son awesomely.

"You 're saying the truth," the monk responded ; "and there 's wonderful news in this letter. It 's not every day that the king has a letter like this."

"It must be a fine thing to be a great man like you," declared Little John.

Robin Hood: His Book

"So it is," agreed the monk. "Still, a great man ought not to be proud, and I'll tell you the word that's in the letter. It's a vast honor you're having, mind you that now."

"And what might be in the letter?" asked William Scarlet, for the sun was sinking lower and lower.

"It's not manners to hurry your betters," said the monk, "but I must get on, so I'll tell you the news. That bold outlaw Robin Hood has been taken, and he is shut up in the lowest dungeon cell of the jail in Nottingham. It's locked and barred and bolted, and so is the outside door, and so is the gate of the jail, and so is the gate of the town, and the jailer's forbid to let any one, save the king himself, through even the outer gate unless the sheriff be with him."

"Truly, that's a mighty piece of news," said Little John, "and it's properly grateful that we are to you for stopping to tell it to simple country folk like us. It's a great thing to bear a letter to the king, and it needs a brave man, too, in these days. I'd not like to be you — saving the dishonor to your Reverence — for I'd fear meeting some of the bold outlaw's followers on the way through the forest. They say there's many a wild fellow that's sworn to do Robin Hood's bidding."

The monk looked fearfully over his right shoulder, then over his left.

"Have you seen any signs of them abroad?" he whispered.

"It's no longer ago than when the sun was overhead that I saw three cloaks, all of the Lincoln green, lying in a roll under a tree not far from here," answered Little John, "and I thought then, thought I, 'Where can Robin be?' They say that when Robin's far away his men go forth all hereabouts in search of him, and I've heard that if he's not to be found, they're that angered, sir, that they kill every man they come across."

The great-headed monk began to tremble.

"You are three strong men," said he, "and I'm only one, for the page would be but a coward if he saw a shadow. Will you not go through the forest with me? I'll give you each a silver penny when you've seen me safely through. You're not outlaws yourselves, are you?" he asked suspiciously. "You're not masterless men, are you, perchance?"

"We be the truest servants that ever a master had in all Yorkshire," declared William Scarlet.

So they rode on until they were in the deepest part of the forest. Then asked Much the miller's son : —

"What will they do with Robin ?"

"They 'll hang him, of course," answered the monk comfortably; "and I 'd not wonder at all if when the king reads the letter, he should send five-score good stout men-at-arms to carry the knave away to London, so that all the land can see him when he 's a-hanging on the gallows-tree. It 's hanging that he deserves, for he stole one hundred silver pounds from me myself once upon a time."

"And are you not sorry to take a man's life for a bit of silver ? " asked William Scarlet.

"Not I," answered the monk flatly. His courage was rising, for he began to see the light through the trees on the farther side of the forest, and he added: "I 've no fear of Robin or his men, and I 'd not be afraid to meet any number of them. I 'd hit one man with my right hand and one with my left, and they 'd fall down like ninepins round about me."

"Then strike!" cried Little John. He seized the monk by the throat, and pulled him down to the ground. He gave one blow with his sharp sword, and the monk's great head rolled off down the hill and through the vale. It may be that it's rolling yet, for no one ever saw it stop.

"That's not all," said Little John. "It's not right to keep the king's letter from him. We must find it and send it to him in London town."

So they all began to search for the king's letter, but it was nowhere to be found. They tore up the monk's hood, and they cut his cloak into slits with their swords, and they even poked their fingers into the very ends of his long-toed shoes, but they could not find the letter to the king.

"Where's the page?" cried William Scarlet suddenly. "We'll have to kill him, or he'll tell the sheriff."

They all stopped searching for the letter, and began to look for the boy. He sat on his horse under a tree not far away, and he was laughing so that he almost rolled off to the ground. Little

John drew his sword and strode up to him, but the boy only laughed the more. Little John looked puzzled.

" It 's not well-mannered to cut a man's head off till he 's had his laugh out," said he ; and so he stood patiently by and waited. It seemed as if the boy never would have his laugh out. He giggled and he tittered and he chuckled, and he held on to his sides as if they would burst. He rubbed his hands, he bounced up and down in the saddle, he swung back and forth until the tears ran down his cheeks, and still he kept bursting into such mighty guffaws of laughter that no one would have thought they could come from so slender a laddie. All this while Little John stood patiently waiting for him to have his laugh out. At last the boy stopped from sheer exhaustion, and Little John said : —

" It 's not good manners to ask too many questions, but would you mind telling me what you were laughing at ? "

" To see you three simpletons a-hunting for the letter," replied the boy, with a giggle.

" What do you know of the letter? " they all cried together.

" Here it is," said the boy; and he pulled it out of his bosom.

" What is the stone tied to it for? " demanded Much the miller's son.

" To make it sink, of course," replied the boy. " You three be such noodles."

" Where did you get the letter? " asked Little John quickly, for the boy seemed ready to go off into another burst of laughter.

" Where could I get it but out of the monk's hood? " said he. " I rode up behind him, and I slipped it out of his hood, and I tied a stone to it, and I was going to drop it over my shoulder when we forded the river. Master Robin 's been good to us, he has; and it was to my own sister that he gave a hundred pounds for a dowry."

" That lad's head is too good to be wasted," declared Little John. " Will you stay with us, boy, and live in the forest, or will you go back to Nottingham and be a page to the sheriff? You shall choose freely for yourself, and no one shall say you nay."

" In faith, I 'll stay with you," declared the boy heartily, " and I 'll do all that a boy can do to save Master Robin from the gallows-tree."

" Will you go with me to bear the letter to the king? " asked Little John.

" That will I," answered the boy; so, while Much the miller's son and William Scarlet went back through the forest to make their way toward Nottingham, Little John smoothed out the letter, and mounted the horse of the great-headed monk, and he and the boy went bravely on to the palace of the king.

At the gate of the palace Little John knocked loud with the hilt of his sword.

" Who 's there? " called the gate-keeper.

" The bearer of a letter to the king from the sheriff of Nottingham," answered Little John.

" Enter," cried the gate-keeper; and the gate was swung wide open.

Little John and the page were led to the great door of the king's hall. There sat the king on his throne, and beside him sat the queen.

" A messenger with a letter from the sheriff of Nottingham," cried the herald.

" A welcome to the bearer of a letter from my faithful servant," said the king graciously; but to the queen he whispered: —

"That fellow is forever telling me that some-body's done something. Can't he let a king alone once in a while?"

Little John walked boldly up to the throne and knelt on one knee.

"God save my liege king," said he, and he presented the letter from the sheriff of Not-tingham.

The king read a few lines. He looked first at the scroll, and then at Little John.

"But where is the monk that was to have brought the letter?" he asked.

"Truly, Sir King, he died before my eyes; but the little page told me where to find the letter. He said it was to be borne to the king, so for the lack of a better messenger I even made shift to bear it myself."

"Are you in service?" asked the king.

"Yes, Sir King," answered Little John, "and to as good a man as ever trod the soil of England. He would have brought the letter himself only too gladly, but he went to hear mass at the church this morning, and he 'd not yet come back."

"Right," said the king approvingly. "Tell your master that if ever he wants a friend he will find one in his sovereign. Ask him from his king to give you a holiday, and here's twenty silver pounds to divide between you and the little page. Write to the sheriff," he bade his scribe, "and say that I am grateful for his faithfulness, and he shall not lack advancement. Say to him that so bold an outlaw as the one now in his prison must come before the king for judgment of his many crimes. Bid him, therefore, send the man called Robin Hood to me with as large an escort as he may deem sufficient for his safe conduct."

The letter was written and sealed with the royal seal. Again Little John and the page louted low before the king, and then they set out for Nottingham.

When they were out of sight, the king whispered to the queen : —

" Robin 's the bravest fellow in the whole land, and I 'd give half the jewels in my crown to catch him."

" And I 'd give the other half to set him free," whispered the queen.

" Sh!" said the king, more softly than ever. " Just let me get him safe in my prison, and we 'll see what we 'll see. I 've a man that knows when to slip a bolt one side and when to forget to turn a key."

The king and the queen laughed together on the throne like two children; then they rose and walked down the hall, and entered the royal dining-room with all the dignity that one ought to have who wears a purple velvet robe and a crown full of jewels.

Little John and the page rode to Nottingham as fast as their horses could carry them. They knocked on the gate, and shouted, " A messenger with a letter from the king to the sheriff!" but there were so many locks and bars and bolts that it was a long time before the gate-keeper could open to them.

" And why are the gates fastened so tight?" asked Little John. " Are the Frenchmen coming to take the land?"

" No, but there's a bold outlaw down in the lowest dungeon of the jail," answered the gate-keeper, "and the sheriff sits and trembles for fear his men will get into the city and carry off the prisoner."

" Which is the way to the sheriff's house?" asked Little John.

" It 's down this road a bit, then up the next, then turn to the right, and you 'll see the sheriff's house; and very like the sheriff himself will be sitting on the steps looking toward the jail, he 's so fearful that the man will be stolen away before his eyes."

Little John and the page went to the sheriff's house and gave him the letter with the king's seal.

" And where is the monk that should have brought the letter ? " demanded the sheriff of the little page. " Was it not you that set out with him ? "

" Surely," answered the little page, "but when it was time to come back, the king gave the letter to this man, and I did not see the monk any-where about. Might it be that the king has made him Abbot of Westminster or Archbishop of Canterbury ? "

" It might well be," said the sheriff, holding his head high in the air. " It would be only fair to do honor to my messenger when he bears such tidings as that. And what shall I give you for a reward ? " asked he of Little John; and Little John replied thoughtfully : —

" It was once that I was crossing a footbridge,

and I had a bit fight with a man. I'd like well to know if that man was Robin Hood. It's something for a lad to boast of if he's had a fight with an outlaw like him and gotten the best of it. Would you be willing, sir, to give me just one wee look at him in his dungeon cell?"

"That will I," said the sheriff heartily. "I'd like to have a look at him myself, and make sure that he's not gotten away from us."

The sheriff and Little John went to the prison. The jailer unchained and unbarred and unlocked and unbolted, and before long they were inside the walls. Then they went down and down and down, till they came to the lowest dungeon of all, and there was Robin bound fast with three stout ropes, and every rope tied in seven twisted knots.

"Is that the man you fought with?" asked the sheriff.

"That's the man himself," answered Little John, "and glad am I to see him."

"Then," said the sheriff, "we'll go home to my house, and I'll give you the best wine there is in my cellar, and to-morrow you shall go with me to the king's court, and you shall see the hanging of the wicked outlaw that's shot many and many a one of the king's good red deer."

They went to the sheriff's house, and they drank ale and they drank beer and they drank wine, and at last they went to bed.

Now while the sheriff was sound asleep, drunken with his wine and his ale, Little John was wider awake than ever he had been before in all his life. As soon as the house was still, he slipped out of his room and out of the front door and around the square in the shadow of the houses, and away up the lonely road till he came to the jail.

" Jailer, Jailer," he called softly, and the jailer came to the little window in the wall.

" What is it ? " he whispered.

" Did you know that Robin Hood had got loose ? Come down here, and I 'll help you get away, so you won't be hanged instead of the bold outlaw."

Then the jailer came down and opened the gates and stood in the moonlight all white and trembling.

" How ever could he do it ? " asked he, his teeth chattering with fear.

" That is easy to tell," quoth Little John. " Look at the gates all wide open," — and the jailer was so frightened that he actually forgot that he had just opened them himself.

" Run for your life," whispered Little John. " I 'll tell no one which way you went."

The jailer ran for his life, and Little John quietly picked up the jailer's bunch of keys. He unlocked all the doors and went down, down, down, till he came to the lowest dungeon cell of all, and there lay Robin bound with three stout ropes, and every rope tied in seven twisted knots. In a minute Robin had a good sword in his hand, and the three ropes were cut. He and Little John did not stop to make their way through the city gate, but where the wall was lowest, they leaped down; and there stood the little page in the shadow of the wall, waiting for them with three good horses, and they all went together to the greenwood.

In the morning, at the first crowing of the cock, the sheriff went to the prison, and when he saw that the doors were open and the prisoner was gone, he made a great outcry all through the town. He rang the alarm bell, and offered

Robin Hood : His Book

half his money to any one that would bring in Robin.

"Never shall I dare to come before the king," he moaned. "There is n't another man in the land that he 'd rather see hanged than Robin Hood, and now that the knave 's got free, I 'm woefully afraid the king 'll hang me instead of him."

So the sheriff groaned and lamented, until he was so ill that he had to go to bed and have the surgeon come to bleed him; and all this time Robin was in merry Sherwood Forest, and he and his men were feasting and shouting for joy that Robin was safe again.

When word was brought to the king that Robin was free, he looked very stern.

"Tell the sheriff of Nottingham," said he, "never to say word to me again of the crimes of Robin Hood. Bid him, if ever again he should catch the bold outlaw, to send him straight to me, that I may work my will upon him." The king thought long and seriously, then he added with a very grave face: —

"Yes, you may say that out of my great mercy I have decided that this time he shall not be hanged for his carelessness."

Robin Hood: His Book

The sheriff's messengers went slowly down the road to Nottingham ; while the king turned to the queen and whispered : —

"If I were as good a fellow as Robin, maybe my men would be as true to me as his are to him. If he ever comes into my hands, we know what we 'll do with him, don't we ? "

The king and the queen laughed together like two children. Then they rose and walked down the hall, and entered the royal dining-room with all the dignity that one ought to have who wears a purple velvet robe and a crown full of jewels.

XVI

ROBIN AND MAID MARIAN

ET you back to your bower. Say you no word and think you no thought of the outlaw, for never shall daughter of mine be bride to a man that has neither rent nor fee nor castles nor lands."

"Rent and fee would he have, had not his stewart proved false," said the maiden. "Broad lands and more than one strong castle would be his own, had he not given all to help his friends that were in direst need."

"It's naught to me where they've gone," declared the earl. "He has them not, and that's enough. He'll one day die on the gallows-tree, and that's more than enough. Get you back to your bower."

So said the proud earl to his daughter, the fairest maid in all the North Countree. Then he thought: —

Robin Hood: His Book

"There are more than four-score men that are sworn to do his bidding. One must be friendly to the man that wields the swords. A little waiting may work wonders. Who knows how soon the sheriff will run down the fox?" Therefore to Robin he said:—

"The girl's but young. She knows not one youth from another, save that one has eyes of brown and one has eyes of blue. Go you back to the forest and bide a while. A man of honor will wait till a maid's of fit age to tell her own mind."

This was why Robin Hood went back to the forest without saying another word to his dearest love; and this is why the fairest maid in all the North Countree drew fast the silken curtains of her bower and wept and wept for Robin.

"Wipe your eyes, my own dear child," said her old nurse. "Why he's gone is more than I may tell you, but I've seen more than one youth in my time, and I promise you well that some day you'll see Master Robin coming for you; so make not your eyes red with weeping nor your voice harsh with sobbing. Sew up your silken seam and wait in patience for him that will come."

Then Maid Marian wiped her eyes and took up the silken seam, but ever she sat by the window that looked toward the forest.

The days went on, and every morning the good nurse would say, " Maid Marian, it might be that he would come to-day; " and every night she would say, " Maid Marian, his coming 's one day the nearer."

Still Robin did not come, for in his own mind he said : —

" None shall ever say that the outlaw without castle or lands or rent or fee stole away the love of the fairest maid in all the North Countree."

Maid Marian still sat by the window that looked toward the forest, and she saw not a glimpse and she heard not a sound, when up the broad road on the farther side of the castle came a lord of high degree. His men-at-arms followed him. His banners waved, and the white plume on his helmet shone in the sunlight as he knocked at the castle gate. The gates were flung wide open, and the earl gave him most hearty greeting, for he thought : —

" A lord like him comes not to my castle for

naught. It may be that what I have looked for will now come to pass."

Then did the earl send a page to his daughter's bower, and the page was to say : —

" Lady Marian, dress you in your silks and velvets and cloth of silver and cloth of gold. Put pearls about your neck and diamonds around your wrists, and rubies and emeralds on your lily white fingers, for a lord of high degree 's to feast with us this day."

" O Nurse, Nurse, what ever shall I do?" sobbed Maid Marian. " I know well he 's come to marry me, and I 'll marry no man but Robin."

" Trust your old nurse, my bonny one," said the old woman. " A maid must ever obey her father; so put on your silks and your satins and your gems, and go you to the feast. Sit you at the head of the table, and show all courtesy to your father's guest, as is fitting ; but there 's one thing the earl has forgot. He told you to put on your velvets and your diamonds, but never did he bid you to speak to the lord of high degree. Do just as your father bade you, but for love of Robin, say you not a word to the earl or to the lord of high degree or even to the serving-men, and speak you not a word to any one for the three hours before the time that is set for the feasting. Trust the rest to the old nurse, who loves her child better than her own life."

Then Maid Marian smiled and made herself ready for the feast, and never a word did she say even when the tiring-maid put upon her wrist a bracelet of emeralds instead of a bracelet of diamonds.

The page came to the bower and said, " Lady Marian, the feast is served." Then Lady Marian went graciously to the door of the great hall and took her own place at the head of the table. She smiled upon her father, and she smiled upon the lord of high degree, but never a word did she speak. The earl slipped away from the room and called the nurse and demanded to know what this might mean.

" Indeed, Master, it is wondrous strange," declared the nurse, " but not a word has she spoken since the tiring-woman began to robe her for the feast. Might she be struck dumb, sir? There are greater deeds than that done by witchcraft. My own father had an uncle who—" but the earl would wait for no stories of witchcraft. He went back to the feasting, and he found, much to his surprise, that all was well. Maid Marian smiled and made signs to the serving-men to do what she would have them, and as for the lord of high degree, he was talking to her earnestly, and looking as happy as a man can look who sees all things going according to his will.

When the Lady Marian had gone to her bower, the lord of high degree said to the earl: —

"Your daughter is marvellous fair, Sir Earl."

"I find her face pleasant to look upon," answered the earl, "and this trouble which has but to-day come upon her, will, I trust, soon pass away."

"What trouble mean you, Sir Earl?"

"That she is dumb, my lord. But truly the illness showed itself only this morning."

"I had not marked it," said the lord of high degree; and indeed he had been so busy talking to the maiden fair that he had not noticed that she never spoke in return. "It is naught. I want a wife to sit at the head of my table, to wear silks and satins and jewels many and rare.

Robin Hood : His Book

Whether your daughter is dumb or not is nothing. Will you give her to me to wife?"

"Yes," answered the earl. "She shall marry you in a week."

"Why not in the morning?" asked the lord of high degree.

"In the morning, if so you say," declared the earl.

Then the earl sent a page to his daughter to say:—

"To-morrow at noon you are to marry the lord of high degree."

"O Nurse, Nurse," sobbed the maiden, "what shall I do? My father bids me wed the lord of high degree, and, indeed, I'll wed no man but Robin."

The nurse had been so sure that no lord of high degree would wish for a dumb bride that she knew not what to say; and she, too, began to weep and to wring her hands for grief at the sorrow of her nursling.

Suddenly Maid Marian wiped her eyes and stood up straight in the middle of the floor.

"Nurse," said she, "are you as sure that Robin wants me for his wife as you are that the sun will rise in the morning?"

" Indeed, I am," said the old nurse earnestly; and she might well be sure, for before he went, Robin had begged her not to let Maid Marian lose thought of him that was far away. " If she knows only the blue eyes from the brown," he had said, " she will forget me in spite of all; but if so be that she does know one youth from another by aught beside the hue of the eyes and the shape of the cloak, then is it only right that she should have one beside her to tell her that my heart is as true as her own."

" Nurse," said Maid Marian, " the lord of high degree may have his wedding in the morning if he will, but another bride must be found, for I shall be neither in the church nor in the castle; and when he mounts his horse for his homeward ride I shall not be beside him."

" You 'll not —" began the old nurse fearfully

" No, Nurse, I 'll not leap from the castle tower, and I 'll not drop into the moat. If I am to lose my life for any man, it will not be for the lord of high degree, it will be for Robin."

Then Maid Marian laid by her silks and her satins and her jewels, and she put upon her a tunic and cloak and sword and buckler.

" Farewell, Nurse," said she. " I 'm going to the forest in search of Robin ; but are you as sure he wants me as you are that the rivers run into the sea ? "

" Truly, I am," answered the old nurse. " But you 'll not go to the forest alone. Wherever you go, I go ;" and nothing that Maid Marian could plead would make her change her mind. " Wherever you go, I go," was all that she would say.

" How can a warrior bold go out into the world and carry his nurse with him ? " asked Maid Marian ; but all that the nurse answered was, " Wherever you go, I go."

" There 's none can go with a knight save a page," declared Maid Marian.

" Then a page I 'll be," said the old nurse. The hour was at hand when the castle gate would be shut for the night, so Lady Marian made the nurse into as good a page as might be in the little time left before the sun would set, and down the narrow path that led to the greenwood walked the strangest knight and page that ever had left the castle keep. Deep into the forest they went. They slept on soft beds of pine needles, and in the morning they feasted on the bread and cheese that they had brought and on the berries that grew by the way.

"I love the life of the forest," said Maid Marian; but the nurse shook her head so that the page's little cap almost fell to the ground.

"Sometimes the forest is kind," said she. "It gives us soft beds, and it gives us sweet berries; but sometimes it is unkind. What shall you do, my brave knight, if the forest brings us a wild beast? Then, too, there are other rangers of the greenwood than Robin. What could you do if a warrior with sword and shield should come upon us? How could you meet him?"

"As one good knight should meet another good knight," declared Maid Marian, laughing gayly. "Many a knightly joust and many a tournament have I seen, and I know more of the sword-play than one would think. Let the knight come, if he will. Here is one to give him a fitting welcome."

Even as she spoke, they saw afar off through the trees one coming toward them in the dress of a knight. His visor was down, and he was ready for warfare. He gave courteous greeting, however, and said, though without lifting his visor: —

" It is the custom of us who dwell in the forest to invite every stranger who passes this way to dine with us."

" Thank you for your invitation, but we wish not to dine," replied Maid Marian ; and she tried so hard to keep her voice from trembling that it was strange and harsh.

" He who enters the forest must yield to the forest customs," said the knight rather curtly. "Will you come with us ? "

" He who abides in a castle follows the customs of the castle," retorted Maid Marian, " and it is not the custom in castles to force an invitation upon an unwilling guest."

" He who enters the forest must yield to the forest customs," repeated the knight. " If you refuse, then fight."

He drew his sword, and Maid Marian drew hers. She had not made an idle boast when she said she knew something of the sword-play. The forester was skilled, but Maid Marian was quick. Long it was that they thrust and they parried, while the old nurse stood wringing her hands and calling upon all the saints to save her nursling. Neither of the fighters heard her, for the blows were falling thick and fast. At last, Maid Marian's sword slipped from her hand, and she sank down on the ground from very weariness. The old nurse screamed : —

"Oh, my darling, my own Lady Marian! Go away!" she cried to the strange knight, pushing him with all her little strength. "You've killed her, you've killed Maid Marian, the fairest maid in all the North Countree."

The strange knight did not go away. Instead of doing that, he pulled off Maid Marian's helmet; then he pulled off his own and ran to the brook for water, and when Maid Marian opened her eyes, the knight was kissing her as if kissing were the only thing that would ever bring her to herself.

Then he told her what the earl had said, and she told him about the lord of high degree. "And he was to be married this noon," said Maid Marian, "and I fear I'll not be there in time to be his bride."

"Would you take me instead?" asked Robin —for of course the strange knight was Robin himself. He asked it very humbly, for no one had yet told him that Maid Marian had come out into the forest not only to run away from the lord of high degree, but because she wanted to find Robin.

" How can one be married without a wedding-gown?" asked Maid Marian. " The maidens of our house do not wed in tunic and cloak, nor do they wear shield and buckler when they go to the altar. Perhaps I'd best go back to my bower." She looked toward Robin, but he had gone down the lane at full speed.

Before Maid Marian and the nurse had hardly time to wonder where he had gone, he was with them again.

" Not far to the eastward," said he, " there lives a knight, Sir Richard at the Lea. He is a good friend to me, and it will gladden the heart of his lady wife to send a wedding-gown for my own Maid Marian."

Soon came a swift messenger with the wedding-gown for Maid Marian, and another gown for the good old nurse. Then they all went down the hill to a tiny village that lay at the edge of the forest. The church was full, and the doors and windows were full, for not only had Robin's men come to the wedding, but all the villagers had left their busy harvesting to see the marriage of their good friend, Master Robin.

The knight and his good wife were there, and it was the knight who gave the bride away.

So it was that the fairest maid in all the North Countree became the true and loving wife of Robin Hood.

www.ingramcontent.com/pod-product-compliance
Lightning Source LLC
Chambersburg PA
CBHW041208100726
47911CB00017B/890